The Flight of the Condor

The Flight
of the Condor

Stories of Violence and
War from Colombia

Translated and compiled by

Jennifer Gabrielle Edwards

Foreword by

Hugo Chaparro Valderrama

The University of Wisconsin Press

The University of Wisconsin Press
1930 Monroe Street, 3rd Floor
Madison, Wisconsin 53711-2059

www.wisc.edu/wisconsinpress/

3 Henrietta Street
London WC2E 8LU, England

1   3   5   4   2

Printed in the United States of America

Library of Congress Cataloging-in-Publication Data
The flight of the condor: stories of violence and war from Colombia /
translated and compiled by Jennifer Gabrielle Edwards;
foreword by Hugo Chaparro Valderrama.
        p.   cm. — (The Americas)
ISBN 0-299-22360-4 (cloth: alk. paper)
ISBN 0-299-22364-7 (paper: alk. paper)
1. Short stories, Colombian.   2. Colombian fiction—21st century.
3. Violence—Fiction.   I. Edwards, Jennifer Gabrielle.
II. Chaparro Valderrama, Hugo.   III. Series: Americas (Madison, Wis.)
        PQ8173.F55   2007
    863'.01089861—dc22   2007011784

For
JUANFER,
compañero de viaje

In Italy for 30 years under the Borgias they had warfare, terror, murder, bloodshed, but they produced Michelangelo, Leonardo De Vinci, and the Renaissance. In Switzerland they had brotherly love. They had 500 years of democracy and peace and what did they produce? The cuckoo clock . . .

Orson Welles, The Third Man

Everything proves that human passions have not changed. Moral progress does not exist, . . . the human soul does not transform, and all efforts to domesticate the human beast have been in vain. History is nothing but a constant return to barbarism. It's a physical world that every day becomes truly magical, in which all of the secrets of science are exploited for the benefit of mankind. Sheltered in regal mansions; illuminated with fluorescent light; owner of radios, motor vehicles, and refrigerators; ruler of space and of time; the spirit of the caves remains imperturbable.

Hernando Téllez, Textos no recogidos en libro

Contents

Contents

Contents

Once upon a Time

A Short Story on Violence

Hugo Chaparro Valderrama
Translated by *Jennifer Gabrielle Edwards*

We were predestined: when the coat of arms of the Republic of Colombia was approved in 1834, the symbols that represent the richness of the country were dwarfed by a vulture. With its outspread wings, a laurel wreath in its beak, and a ribbon on which was written "liberty and order," the condor that appears in the upper part of the shield foretold our destiny. In the nineteenth century alone we had, as Gonzalo Sánchez observes, "eight generalized civil wars, fourteen localized civil wars, two foreign wars with Ecuador, and three military coups. It is no accident that the century ended with the War of a Thousand Days, which was at the same time the last war of the nineteenth century and the first of the twentieth."[1]

And it is no accident that Colonel Aureliano Buendía of *One Hundred Years of Solitude* by Gabriel García Márquez is an imaginary biographical sketch of so many real heroes of Colombia, whom stubbornness and hope have never forsaken. For readers outside the country, the novel is a fantastical story; in Colombia, it's the account of a long history in which it is not entirely implausible to assume that the escapades perpetrated by the colonel were true: thirty-two armed uprisings, fourteen offensives, seventy-three ambushes, and the firing squad for anyone who managed to escape; Buendía later survived "enough strychnine in his coffee to kill a horse."[2]

In the face of a reality condemned by war, fiction is a way to comprehend its calamities. Colombian authors have portrayed, in different ways, the events of our civil wars, political battles, and violence.

As melodrama and revolution became narrative themes in Mexico in the 1930s and in Cuba beginning in the 1960s, violence burst into Colombian literature, devastatingly and irrevocably, when conflict was reignited in the late 1940s between the political parties that have historically governed the country: the conservative and the liberal.[3]

The Cross, the Rifle, and Chaos

The soldiers of the War of a Thousand Days, in addition to using their rifles, "protected" themselves from death with religious images hung from their necks. The State and the Church, two decisive forces for the history of Colombia, divided the country at the end of the nineteenth century between the realism and barbarism of weapons, and religious fantasy. The members of the conservative party were fervent Catholics, and the liberals, although not entirely devoid of religion, were designated by the conservatives as their moral enemies. Radicalism and its persecutions heralded one of the great themes of Colombian literature of the twentieth century: the intolerance of those in power.

With the assassination on April 9, 1948, of the liberal leader Jorge Eliécer Gaitán in Bogotá, bitterness and vengeance sowed boundless chaos in the nation. The history of Colombia was divided between a before and an after that dramatically altered coexistence and proliferated deaths in the 1950s. The streets of Bogotá were taken over by an angry mob that exhibited its rage by destroying everything in its path, expressing its frustration through looting, arson, and the transformation of the country's capital into a battlefield where any passerby could become a victim of the snipers. *Bogotazo* was the term that Colombians bequeathed to the future to refer to the crisis of April 9, a major turning point in their history.

The assassination of Jorge Eliécer Gaitán is still a mystery. Aside from the murderer who shot him, the conspirators remain in obscurity.[4] A general who was at President Mariano Ospina Pérez's side when the crisis erupted replied to a writer who interviewed him years later: "I'll go to hell with the truth of what happened that day."[5]

Murder, Inc.

Deaths reached large-scale proportions in the 1950s. Leaders of both the left-wing guerrilla groups and the right-wing armed factions—known as *pájaros* (birds)—christened themselves with novelistic aliases: Capitán Venganza (Captain Vengeance), Sangrenegra (Blackblood), El Cóndor (The Condor), Desquite (Revenge), Pedro Brincos (Jumping Peter), Zarpazo (Claw), Tarzán (Tarzan), Chispas (Sparks), La Gata (The Cat). Structured like a mafia in political code, with liberal and conservative leaders their godfathers, these armed men and women spread their war all over Colombia at the bidding of their supporters. The guerrilla groups were typically allied with the liberal political party, left-wing activists, and peasants, and the *pájaros* enjoyed the support of the conservative political party, the military, and wealthy landowners.

Both guerrillas and *pájaros* felt betrayed when in mid-1958 the two main political parties entered into an agreement known as the National Front, which secured "a new pact among the ruling classes who would now assume responsibility for not only basic economic leadership of the country but also the general leadership of the State and exercise of politics itself."[6]

It was a clever bipartisan strategy that would benefit both the liberal and conservative parties, who agreed to alternate control of the government for sixteen years. As a result, those who had fought at the politicians' behest—guerrillas for the liberals and *pájaros* for the conservatives—and had carried out their bloody orders throughout the 1950s went into hiding. And the State disassociated itself from them, demoting them from patriotic warriors to mere "bandits," thus paving the way for unfettered retribution.

The retribution perpetrated against the guerrilla groups, now without their benefactors' support and protection, was particularly bloody. For many ordinary Colombians who identified with these groups—whether due to ideological conviction, social class, or the accident of geography—the guerrillas were perceived with a mix of horror and admiration and their prolonged battles against their enemies—the *pájaros,* the army, and the National Police—became legendary. Some Colombians, faced with an implausible reality, replaced it with fantasy and its fictions and went so far as to embark on pilgrimages to where guerrillas were buried or killed, to bestow floral tributes in honor of their memory, and to attribute them with magical powers with which they could transform, when the army had them surrounded, into animals or the wind whispering among the troops.[7]

Between History, Literature, and Eyewitness Accounts of a Bewildering Reality

The response of Colombian literature to such an astonishing reality has been to depict it in a no less astonishing way. When the United Fruit Company pressured the government to defend the company's interests during the strike that broke out in the northern Colombian state of Magdalena in October of 1928, the strategy used to control the strikers was to mobilize the army to the town of Ciénaga. In the early morning of December 6 of that same year, the banana workers, gathered in the train station, were killed by the troops. Known as "the banana plantation massacre," the episode was depicted by García Márquez in *One Hundred Years of Solitude*. In the author's fictional retelling of the event he magnified the severity of the massacre to satisfy the aesthetic purposes of his work, and his readers, taking a poetic truth for a literal one, quoted excerpts of the novel as if it were a history book. In the early 1990s García Márquez explained how fiction got in the way of reality:

> People were talking about a massacre. An apocalyptic massacre. It's hard to be sure, but there couldn't have been that many deaths . . . That was a problem for me . . . when I discovered that it wasn't this spectacular bloodbath. In a book like *One Hundred Years of Solitude,* in which everything is magnified, I needed to fill an entire train with dead bodies.[8]

Given the statistics of the civil war that ravaged Colombia from 1946 to 1964, one might assume that the reality of the country was constantly imitating its exaggerated literature. The figures, which range from 80,000 to 400,000 dead, indicate a long nightmare difficult to absorb. Sooner or later, Colombians were going to believe they lived in a novel when they read the news or reflected on the country's almost unbelievable history. They read, for example, newspaper accounts of people living in fantastic circumstances engendered by acts of unprecedented violence, such as the story published in *El Tiempo* on April 13, 1999, about the town with only one resident, Carlos Calvo González, a peasant who decided to stay behind in Payón de Orozco (Magdalena) to look for traces of the victims of a paramilitary massacre. "I want to find them [his wife and brother who had been killed] or any of the thirty dead of that day so they can tell me if it was just me who didn't know that this could happen," he explained. "That's why I keep going to the places where they were gunned down. But it's no use, the dead won't come out."[9]

Another town, another family terrorized, and the characteristically Colombian phantasmagoric tone is also found in this excerpt of a childhood experience from a woman's chronicle published in *Exiled: Chronicles of Displacement* edited by sociologist, writer, and journalist Alfredo Molano:

> I woke up one night, not because of the chickens but because of the gunshots I heard in the street. The shots were very loud and so close that you went to look and see where they were hitting. And especially since it was night, with the echo the streets make. My mom started to cry and say that we were going to be killed and then I ran out to count my chickens, to make sure all of them were there, but they were all dead, suffocated among the tin cans I had used to cover them up so the rats wouldn't eat them. My dad looked at them with all the tin cans and said to my mom that he was afraid the same thing would happen to us. He had already been afraid since the night when the electricity went out and a young boy turned up dead in the center of town. My dad said that his tongue had been cut out with a knife. That they had cut off pieces of his fingers, just like we used to do with the turtles, but he comforted my mom by telling her that that was the last time the paramilitary could leave a dead person like that, because the authority had banned them from killing inside the town. My dad said that now, to kill someone, what they had to do was take him out of town, far away, where his family couldn't find him. I didn't see the dead body, but I heard everything my dad told my mom.[10]

Violence in Long Shot, Fear in Close Up

The writer Hernando Téllez sums up in two of his stories, "Lather and Nothing Else" and "Prelude," how Colombian authors have depicted violence: through personal stories that explain how their characters survive the chaos; and with stories told by protagonists, representing the inhabitants of whole towns or cities, who discover the ubiquitous tragedy of the country. Between the individual and the communal, and the towns and the nation, Téllez's stories' perspectives complement each other as they strive to tackle both the vicissitudes of daily life and the great events of history. In cinematographic terms, it's an image of Colombia in which close-ups alternate with long shots, both equally compelling as means to illustrate, in literary code, the presence of death.

The testimony of different authors writing in various periods of history offers a panorama of styles and visions that defies the simplification of violence. In Álvaro Cepeda Samudio's "The Soldiers," the troops sent by the United Fruit Company to suppress the banana worker strike do not understand or entirely accept their mission. Without venturing a definitive judgment, they wonder why they should become the messengers of death for the strikers. What right do they have to shoot into a crowd of people? Whose fault is a crime: he who orders the murder or he who obeys the order?

The Stevenson metaphor, which suggests that human beings are Dr. Jekylls threatened by Mr. Hydes, is apparent in those stories that try to explain the circumstances of their characters without making them either entirely virtuous or absolutely cruel. In fiction, doubt and its conflicts express García Márquez's idea that there is no such thing as a definitively unilateral human experience. One must understand the point of view of the hare but also that of the hound that pursues it.

In these stories we find variations of the same theme: the political violence that engulfed Colombia from the 1940s to the mid-1960s. We observe the mayor slowly backed into a corner by the captain's questioning in "The New Order" by Arturo Echeverri Mejía, the soldiers compelled by time and history into a forced retirement in

"The Day We Buried Our Weapons" by Plinio Apuleyo Mendoza, political color as ideological symbol that unleashes savagery in "My Father Was Blue" by Nicolás Suescún, and the vultures that devour a town in "The Feast" by Policarpo Varón. The contrasting points of view offered by these and other stories in this collection bring the reader a step closer to more fully comprehending the dimensions of Colombia's story.

Liberty and Order?

Colombia was the setting of a civil war with various protagonists and interests throughout the second half of the twentieth century. After the violence of the 1940s, the war continued as a consequence of the intolerance and arrogance of those in power. The motto of the national coat of arms, liberty and order, was read in different ways depending on ideology, political color, and organized crime. There were many interpretations: In the 1960s the Fuerzas Armadas Revolucionarias de Colombia (Revolutionary Armed Forces of Colombia, or FARC) and the Ejército de Liberación Nacional (National Liberation Army, or ELN) guerrilla groups were formed, followed in the 1970s by another guerrilla group, the M-19, which was behind a long and troubling history of military strikes against the State until 1990, when some of its members reentered civil society. In the 1980s the drug cartels built an empire that ended—symbolically although not definitively—on December 2, 1993, when the police killed Colombia's most famous mafioso, Pablo Escobar Gaviria, who was responsible for a daring criminal enterprise as fantastical as it was sinister. Also formed in the 1980s were the paramilitaries who, like the *pájaros* of the 1950s, were armies that acted at the behest of "politicians, wealthy landowners, narco-landowners, narco-traffickers,[11] the military, the police, and other agents of State security."[12] They were recruited by these groups to kill their adversaries, including guerrillas, liberal politicians, academics, and union activists.

Many factors have contributed to making violence the cliché with which Colombia tends to be identified, disregarding other dimensions of its reality, among them the displacement of whole towns threatened by war, the terrorist strategy of the mafia, the increasing power of the guerrilla groups that utilize drug trafficking and kidnapping to finance themselves, the ongoing war between left-wing guerrillas and right-wing paramilitaries, and the role of a State incapable of putting an end to the brutality.[13]

A Literary Puzzle

The uncertainty of war: "Fear" by Manuel Mejía Vallejo. The crime that exacerbates the neuroses of its perpetrators and witnesses: "The Designator" by Roberto Montes Mathieu. The city and the countryside as settings for the same conflict: "Bitter Sorrows" by Darío Ruiz Gómez. In "Family Birthday Wishes" by Germán Espinosa the cynicism of crime becomes the pretext for a picaresque dialogue. Juan Carlos Botero's "Execution" and Mario Mendoza Zambrano's "A Christmas Story" both manage to reveal the unrest of the country in no more than a macabre snapshot while in "Vendors of Peculiar Objects" by Celso Román the spectacle of violence is portrayed as a delirious and grotesque circus. Violence is at the center of an oblique sexual perversion in Evelio Rosero Diago's "Brides by Night"; Germán Santamaría parodies the ghost story genre in "The Procession of Shadows." All of these stories are fragments of an image of Colombia depicted with different narrative styles and one theme in common: the disequilibrium of a country that is losing its sense of nationhood and revealing itself as a jigsaw puzzle of regions bound together only by accident through Colombian emblems such as its anthem, flag, sports, and coffee.

Outside the confines of politically motivated stories, in which the importance of sociological explanation supersedes that of fiction, some authors have used the primordial fear of death and the frailty of the human condition as ways to understand the limits imposed by the fate of their characters. The literary journey through Colombia's civil wars has advanced toward another dimension, at the same rhythm and with the same impetus as Latin American film. From the great plazas and their waving flags to the slogans and political oratory in the style of the 1960s and '70s, another reality, no less eloquent, has been discovered that shows, through an individual's subjective experience, how a country reacts to its dilemmas. The descriptive tone of violence has been replaced by violence without political color or, simply, fear. Hernando Téllez's lesson has not been in vain.

With different perceptions of the country and its fears, stories like "Gelatin" by Harold Kremer, "The Aroma of Death" by Heriberto Fiorillo, "Eme" by Julio Paredes," and "The Sixth Commandment" by Juan Fernando Merino reject the terms of a generalized anxiety to focus instead on the interior landscape of characters conscious of their frailty. These plots elude literary nationalism: aside from the local color that identifies them as stories that only could have been written in Colombia, they are able to engage a readership outside of the borders of the country through the elemental fears they reveal. "The Sixth Commandment" and "Eme" are stories about growth through experience, revelations, and fate's role in deciding the course of a life in an extreme situation. "Gelatin" and "The Aroma of Death" turn to suspense. In Kremer's story, anguish transforms a salesman into a psychopath; in Fiorillo's, the shock felt upon discovering a victim's body is so tremendous that the motives, when revealed, fail to mitigate the immutability of death.

Once upon a Time

"An empty house falls," says a woman recalling the house from which her daughter, threatened by the paramilitaries, had to escape.[14] The metaphor is useful in understanding how a country, like a house, when abandoned and left to decay, collapses. Colombia has survived the crossfire between guerrillas, the mafia, the paramilitaries, and the army, powers concerned exclusively with their own well-being. The forced displacement of peasants in the midst of a war only allows them to take their lives from one place to another, to settle down where they can or where they're allowed. Hope has thus become a form of resistance, of staving off chaos and refusing to resign oneself to disaster. Colombian literature, in making violence and its depiction a literary genre, reclaims and occupies this house; we can therefore continue finding between its walls solutions for how to survive, without forgetting our ghosts.

Notes

1. Gonzalo Sánchez, "De amnistías, guerras y negociaciones," in Memoria de un país en guerra, ed. Gonzalo Sánchez and Mario Aguilera (Bogotá: Planeta, 2001), 329.

2. Gabriel García Márquez, *Cien años de soledad* (Buenos Aires: Editorial Sudamericana, 1967), 94.

3. "The rapid increase in the production [of coffee] in Colombia and in other coffee-bean–producing countries led to an abrupt fall in international prices during the second half of the 1890s. According to government critics the impact of this decline in Colombia was exacerbated by government economic policy. Such people had in mind not only alleged poor monetary management but also the imposition of tax liability on coffee exports in 1895. It is difficult to determine how much truth there was in these allegations, but the country's economic difficulties did intensify the opposition to the regime of the liberals and the conservative dissidents; the majority of the latter's power base was located in Antioquia, an important coffee-growing region. The dissidents, who took on the name of Historicals, or Historical Conservatives, in opposition to the Nationalists of [Miguel Antonio] Caro [vice president of Colombia, named president after the death of Rafael Nuñez; governed the country from 1894 to 1898], direct heirs of Nuñez [president of Colombia 1880–1882 and 1884–1894] and his National Party, never formally allied themselves with the liberals, but their disillusionment spurred the latter and necessarily weakened the government in Bogotá. Thus few were surprised when, at the end of 1899, liberal militants unleashed a new civil conflict, which lasted approximately three years and contributed, indirectly, toward the loss of Panama. Within the Liberal Party there was a faction that foresaw if not the loss of Panama, then at least some of the terrible effects that the war would surely bring, but the frustrations of that collective ownership had already become too unbearable to make any moves toward appeasement" (David Bushnell, *Colombia: Una nación a pesar de sí misma* (Bogotá: Planeta, 206))].

4. Juan Roa Sierra, Jorge Eliécer Gaitán's alleged murderer, was dragged and lynched by a mob on the streets of Bogotá. The crowd's rage forever silenced this witness of exceptional importance. Curiously, when Roa Sierra's dead body arrived at the morgue, the cadaver wore a ring with the pirate emblem—a skull and bones—and two ties knotted around its neck.

5. Arturo Alape, *El bogotazo: Memorias del olvido* (Bogotá: Planeta, 1987), 17.

6. Gonzalo Sánchez and Donny Meertens, *Bandoleros, gamonales y campesinos: El caso de la violencia en Colombia* (Bogotá: El Áncora, 1983), 40.

7. The military siege and subsequent murder in Bogotá of Efraín González, a liberal guerrilla fighter, made him an emblematic and heroic figure of what was known as "The Violence." In June of 1965 González, hiding out in a house, confronted the army alone in a combat that lasted five hours and was broadcast like a radio series episode to the entire country. The army, which laid siege to him with machine guns, tanks, hundreds of soldiers, police officers, and secret police, had to fire 70,000 shots to defeat him. The crowd that gathered there supported González and yelled at the soldiers "murderers!" His body was buried, by order of the State, in the south of the country. "By official order, his mother and relatives were not even permitted to attend the burial" (Sánchez and Meertens, *Bandoleros, gamonales y campesinos,* 117).

8. Marco Palacios and Frank Safford, *Colombia: País fragmentado, sociedad dividida* (Bogotá: Grupo Editorial Norma, 2002), 522.

9. Roberto Llanos, "El pueblo con un solo habitante," *El Tiempo* (Bogotá), April 13, 1999, 11a.

10. Alfredo Molano, *Desterrados: Crónicas del desarraigo* (Bogotá: El Áncora, 2001), 45.

11. During the apogee of power of drug cartels in Colombia in the 1980s, the language of everyday Colombians, particularly in the major cities, came to reflect this dominant culture. Thus a whole nomenclature was developed to refer to such things as the ostentatious mansions the drug lords owned (*narco-casas* [narco-houses]) and the SUVs the drug lords drove *(narco-Toyotas);* drug lords who owned land were *narco-latifundistas* (narco-landowners).

12. Palacios and Safford, *Colombia,* 666.

13. If crime doesn't pay, it certainly sells. The thriller genre, both cinematographic and literary, proves it. In Colombia's case, the literature that makes it possible to analyze and understand—or try to understand—the history of a country able to survive, sometimes inexplicably, its political crises is also an export product. During the height of the mafia in the 1980s and '90s, graffiti was written on the walls of Bogotá, adopted by its inhabitants as a declaration of principles: El país se derrumba y yo voy de rumba (The country falls and I'm going out to have a ball). In other words, rather than giving in to the tragedy one must find an escape from the chaos. In a sense, David Bushnell expressed this when writing on the subject of the folklore of patriotism: "The professional cyclists and the novelists, and Juan Valdez and his family looking after their coffee plantation will still be there when the total anachronism of the guerrilla war is finally eliminated and the narcotic trends of the world demand new substances, which Colombia would be in a less favorable position to commercialize" (Bushnell, Colombia, 380).

14. *Una casa sola se vence* (An Empty House Falls) (2004) is the title of a documentary produced by Marta Rodríguez and Fernando Restrepo about the violence and displacement in Colombia in the 1990s. It is part of a trilogy that also includes *Nunca más* (2001) and *Soraya, amor no es olvido* (2006).

Acknowledgments

Special thanks to Juan Fernando Merino for his unflagging support, patient editing of the translation, and scouring of used bookstalls in Bogotá; thanks also to the rest of the Merino family in Cali, especially Doña Fabiola, Mapy, Fernando, Lucho, and "El Capitán" for instilling in me a passion for Colombia that ultimately translated into this ten-year project. Thanks to Harold Kremer for tracking down the authors and their heirs all over Colombia; special thanks to Ilan Stavans for pushing this project forward and to my agent Leylha Ahuile for taking on a literary translator, of all things; to Gwen Walker and Matt Levin at the University of Wisconsin Press for being so helpful and responsive; to Larry Goldstein, editor of *Michigan Quarterly Review,* for his generous hand-written notes in response to my first translations that encouraged me to keep at it; to the authors of these marvelous stories; and to Mom, Dad, Jeremy, and Mary.

Grateful acknowledgment is made for permission to publish the English translations of the following copyrighted works:

Juan Carlos Botero, "La ejecución," in *Las semillas del tiempo* (Bogotá: Planeta, 1992). Reprinted by permission of the author.
Álvaro Cepeda Samudio, "Los soldados," in *La casa grande* (Bogotá: Ediciones Mito, 1962). Reprinted by permission of the publisher.

Arturo Echeverri Mejía, "El nuevo orden," in *Marea de ratas* (Medellín, Colombia: Aguirre Editores, 1960). Reprinted by permission of the Estate of Arturo Echeverri Mejía.

Germán Espinosa, "Telefonema familiar," in *Cuentos completos* (Bogotá: Arango Editores, 1998). Reprinted by permission of the author.

Heriberto Fiorillo, "Aroma de muerte," in *Narradores colombianos en U.S.A.*, ed. Eduardo Márceles Daconte (Bogotá: Instituto Colombiano de Cultura, 1993). Reprinted by permission of the author.

Harold Kremer, "Gelatina," *El Malpensante Magazine* (July–August 1998). Reprinted by permission of the author.

Manuel Mejía Vallejo, "Miedo," in *Cuentos de zona tórrida* (Medellín, Colombia: Editorial Carpel-Antorcha, 1967). Reprinted by permission of the Estate of Manuel Mejía Vallejo.

Plinio Apuleyo Mendoza, "El día que enterramos las armas," in *El desertor* (Bogotá: Editorial Oveja Negra, 1985). Reprinted by permission of the author.

Mario Mendoza Zambrano, "Cuento de Navidad," in *La horrible noche: Relatos de violencia y guerra en Colombia*, ed. Peter Schultze-Kraft (Bogotá: Planeta Colombiana Editorial, 2001). Reprinted by permission of the publisher.

Juan Fernando Merino, "El sexto mandamiento," in *Las visitas ajenas* (Cali, Colombia: Gerencia para el Desarrollo Cultural, 1994). Reprinted by permission of the author.

Roberto Montes Mathieu, "El señalador," in *El cuarto bate* (Bogotá: Plaza & Janés, 1985). Reprinted by permission of the author.

Julio Paredes, "Eme," in *Salón Júpiter (y otros cuentos)* (Bogotá: Tercer Mundo Editores, 1994). Reprinted by permission of the author.

Celso Román, "Vendedores de objetos insólitos," in *Cuentistas bogotanos,* ed. Carlos Nicolás Hernández (Bogotá: Panamericana Editorial, 1999). Reprinted by permission of the author.

Evelio Rosero Diago, "Novias de noche," in *Las esquinas más largas* (Bogotá: Panamericana Editorial, 1998). Reprinted by permission of the author.

Acknowledgments

Darío Ruiz Gómez, "Penas amargas," in *Para que no se olvide su nombre* (Medellín, Colombia: Editorial Universidad de Antioquia, 1966). Reprinted by permission of the author.

Germán Santamaría, "La procesión de los ardientes," in *No morirás* (Bogotá: Editorial Oveja Negra, 1992). Reprinted by permission of the author.

Nicolás Suescún, "Mi padre era azul," in *El extraño y otros cuentos* (Bogotá: Valencia Editores, 1980). Reprinted by permission of the author.

Hernando Téllez, "Preludio" and "Espuma y nada más," in *Cenizas para el viento* (Bogotá: Áncora Editores, 1984). Reprinted by permission of the Estate of Hernando Téllez.

Policarpo Varón, "El festín," in *El festín* (Medellín, Colombia: Editorial Oveja Negra, 1973). Reprinted by permission of the author.

In addition I am grateful for permission to reproduce the following works, whose English translations previously appeared in print:

Julio Paredes, "Eme," trans. Jennifer Gabrielle Edwards, *Metamorphoses* 10, no. 2 (Fall 2002).

Evelio Rosero Diago, "Brides by Night" (originally titled "Novias de noche"), trans. Jennifer Gabrielle Edwards, *Michigan Quarterly Review* 38, no. 2 (Spring 1999).

Hernando Téllez, "Lather and Nothing Else" (originally titled "Espuma y nada más"), trans. Jennifer Gabrielle Edwards, *Metamorphoses* 10, no. 2 (Fall 2002).

The Flight of the Condor

Lather and Nothing Else

Hernando Téllez

He didn't greet anyone when he came in. I was sharpening my best razor. And when I saw him I began to tremble. But he didn't notice. I continued to sharpen the razor to hide my alarm. Then I tested it against the tip of my thumb and held it up to the light again. He was removing his bandolier, with its holster dangling. He hung it on one of the nails in the wardrobe and placed his kepi on top. He turned around to address me and, undoing his tie, said, "It's hot as hell. Give me a shave." And he sat in the chair.

I estimated it had been four days since he had last shaved. The four days the latest expedition to hunt down our people had lasted. His face appeared sunburned, hardened by the sun. I prepared the foam meticulously. I cut a few slices off the bar of soap and let them fall into the bowl. I added a little warm water and stirred it with the brush. It soon began to lather.

"The troops must need a shave as bad as I do."

I kept on beating the lather.

"But, you know what? It was a success. We got the leaders. Some we brought back dead, some are still alive. But soon they'll all be dead."

"How many did you get?" I asked.

"Fourteen. We had to go in pretty far to find them. But they're paying for it now. And not one of them will come out alive, not one."

He leaned back in the chair when he saw I was holding up the shaving brush, full of lather. I still hadn't put the sheet on him.

That's how disoriented I was. I took a sheet out of the drawer and tied it around my client's neck. He didn't stop talking. He took for granted that I was on the side of the new order.

"The town has learned its lesson from what happened the other day," he said.

"Yes," I replied, as I finished tying the knot on his dark, sweaty neck.

"That was pretty good, wasn't it?"

"Very good," I answered, as I picked up the brush again.

The man closed his eyes, sighing with fatigue, and waited for the cool caress of the soap. I had never had him so close. The day he ordered the townspeople to gather in the schoolyard to see the four rebels hanging there, I caught a glimpse of him. But the sight of the mutilated bodies kept my eyes from lingering on the face of the man who was responsible for it all, the man whose face I was now going to take in my hands. It wasn't an unpleasant face, for sure. And his beard, though it made him appear older, looked good on him. His name was Torres. Captain Torres. A man with a good imagination; after all, it hadn't occurred to anyone before him to string up the rebels naked and use various parts of their bodies for target practice.

I started to apply the first layer of soap. His eyes were still closed.

"What I wouldn't do for a little sleep," he said. "But there's a lot of work to be done this afternoon."

I lifted the brush and, feigning casual unconcern, asked, "Firing squad?"

"Something like that, but slower," he replied.

"All of them?"

"No. Just a few."

I returned to the task of lathering his beard. My hands began to shake. The man couldn't have noticed, which was a relief. But I wished he hadn't come. Many of our people had probably seen him come in. And having the enemy on your home turf imposes certain conditions. I'd have to shave that beard like any other, with the greatest care and as if he were my best customer, making sure that not one drop of blood emerged from his pores. Making sure that the razor would not get caught in the little clumps of hair. Making sure that his skin would come out clean, taut, and smooth, and that when I brushed the back of my hand against it, not one hair could be felt on its surface. Yes. I was a clandestine revolutionary, but I was also a barber of integrity, proud of the diligence with which I practiced my profession. And that four-day-old beard needed a lot of work.

I picked up the razor, opened the two handles at an angle, opened the blade, and began my task, heading downward from one of his temples. The blade responded impeccably. His beard was stubborn and hard, not very long, but dense. Little by little, his skin began to appear. The blade emitted its usual sound, and lumps of soap mixed with little hairs accumulated on it. I paused to clean and then sharpen it because I'm a barber who does things right. The man had been keeping his eyes shut. Now he opened them, lifted his hand from underneath the sheet, touched the part of his face that had become free of soap, and said, "Come to the school at six this evening."

"The same as the other day?" I asked, horrified.

"It might be even better," he replied.

"What are you planning on doing?"

"I don't know yet, but it'll be fun." He leaned back again and closed his eyes. I approached with the razor poised.

"Do you plan on punishing all of them?" I ventured timidly.

"All of them."

The soap on his face was drying. I had to get started. I looked out onto the street through the mirror. The same as always: the corner store and two or three customers inside. Then I looked at the clock: 2:20 p.m. The blade continued its descent. Now the other temple and down the cheek. A dark beard, thick. He should let it grow, like some poets and priests do. It would look good on him. Many people wouldn't recognize him. And that would be in his best interest, I thought, as I gingerly moved the blade up his neck. That's where I had to be most careful, since the growth, although still in its early stages, was clumping. A curly beard. The tiny pores could open and release their pearls of blood. The pride of a good barber like me hinges on not letting this happen to any client. And this was an important client. How many of our people had he ordered killed? How many had he ordered mutilated? Better not to think about it. Torres didn't know that I was his enemy. He didn't know and neither did the others. It was a secret known to very few, precisely so that I could inform the revolutionaries about what Torres was up to in the town, and what he planned on doing each time he set out on an incursion to hunt them down. Needless to say, it was going to be very difficult to explain how I had had him at my mercy and then let him go, alive and shaved.

The beard had almost completely disappeared. He looked younger, as if years had been taken off since he came in. I suppose this is what always happens to men when they've been to the barber's. Torres was rejuvenated at the stroke of my razor, yes, because I'm a good barber, the best in this town, and I don't say this out of vanity. A little more soap here, under the chin, over the Adam's apple, on that major artery.

It's so hot! Torres must be sweating too. But he's not afraid. He's serene, not even worried about what he's going to do with the prisoners this afternoon. I, on the other hand, with this razor in my hand, scraping and scraping this skin, making sure that blood doesn't spill from those pores, wary of each stroke, cannot think calmly. Damn him for coming; I am a revolutionary but I am not a murderer. And to think how easy it would be to kill him. And he deserves it.

Does he? No; what the hell! No one is worth the sacrifice of becoming a murderer. What could be gained from it? Nothing. Others come along, and then others, and the first ones kill the second ones and they kill the third group, and it goes on and on until everything is a sea of blood. I could cut this neck like this: Jab! Jab! I wouldn't give him time to protest and since his eyes are closed he wouldn't see the glint of the blade or the glint in my eyes. But I'm shaking like a real murderer. From that neck, a torrent of blood would spurt onto the sheet, onto the chair, onto my hands, onto the floor. I'd have to shut the door. And the blood would keep flowing along the floor, warm, indelible, uncontainable, out into the street, like a thin, scarlet stream. I am sure that a hard jab, a deep incision, would be painless. He wouldn't suffer. And what would I do with the body? Where could I hide it? I'd have to flee, leave all of this, take refuge far away, very far. But they'd hunt me until they found me. "The man who murdered Captain Torres. He slit his throat while giving him a shave. A coward." Or, "The man who avenged our people. A name to remember (fill in my name). He was the town barber. No one knew that he supported our cause. . . . "

So, which is it? Murderer or hero? My destiny hinges on the blade of this razor. I can push down a little more on my hand, lean on the blade just a little, and plunge it in. The skin would give way like silk, like rubber, like sheepskin. There is nothing more tender than a man's skin and the blood is always there, ready to flow. A razor like this does not let you down. It's my best razor. But I don't want to be a murderer, no sir. You came for a shave. And I will do my duty honorably. . . . I don't want to be stained with blood. By lather, and nothing else. You're an executioner and I'm only a barber. Each in his place. That's it. Each in his place.

His face was now clean, smooth, and taut. The man sat up to look at himself in the mirror. He rubbed his skin with his hands and felt it fresh and like new.

"Thank you," he said. He headed toward the wardrobe to get his belt, gun, and kepi. I must have been very pale and my shirt felt soaked. Torres buckled his belt, put his gun back in its holster, ran a hand over his hair mechanically, and put on his kepi. He took a few coins out of his pocket to pay me for my services. Then he started to walk toward the door. He paused in the doorway for a moment, turned around, and spoke.

"They told me that you'd kill me. I came to find out for myself. But killing isn't easy. I know what I'm talking about."

And he headed down the street.

The Execution

Juan Carlos Botero

The guerillas had been fleeing through the jungle for days. There were fifteen left of the original twenty involved in the ambush. They were exhausted and they knew that they still had a week of arduous walking ahead of them. They camped on a riverbank at sunset. That night they confronted their situation: the nine captured soldiers slowed down their retreat, and they didn't have enough provisions to feed them. After a long discussion, the guerillas decided to shoot the soldiers. They led the soldiers to the riverbank with their hands tied behind their backs. In the darkness they looked like frightened children. To save ammunition, they decided to eliminate them in groups of three. They lined up the first group, each man very close behind the other, but the young men didn't seem to understand what was going on. A woman stood in front of the first soldier; she placed her gun against the forehead of the young man, who looked at her with incredulous eyes of terror, and she fired. The heads exploded like green apples. They tossed the cadavers into the river. Slowly, tumbling, the bodies were carried away by the current. The second group shrieked and cursed the guerillas but was killed just the same. They lined up the last three soldiers and the woman pointed her gun at the sweaty forehead of the first and squeezed the trigger. There was a clicking sound. No one laughed. The woman, very serious, reloaded the gun as the soldiers cried hysterically, imploring her not to kill them. She again placed the gun against the soldier's forehead and fired. All three collapsed in the blast. After a few seconds the last soldier realized that he was still alive. His comrade's skull had exploded in his face but the bullet had not reached him. He kept his eyes closed, holding his breath, aware that the hot mass trickling down his eyelids, nose, and mouth was the brain of his friend. Amidst a strange silence, he felt the guerillas picking him up by his shoulders and feet, and he was thrown into the river with the others.

The Soldiers

Álvaro Cepeda Samudio

In this story, Álvaro Cepeda Samudio, one of the most brilliant and in-novative writers Colombian literature has ever produced, tackles one of the most tragic and documented events in Colombia's political history: the so-called banana plantation massacre, when army troops put a bloody end to the strike of the United Fruit Company workers.

According to the history books, dozens of plantation workers were killed as a result of this violent repression; however, in a famous passage in Gabriel García Márquez's One Hundred Years of Solitude, *these dozens become thousands as the author conjures interminable trainloads of victims. In "The Soldiers," Cepeda Samudio approaches these events from a point of view different from his friend and collaborator García Márquez: the events are narrated from the perspective of the government soldiers who set out to finish off the strikers and whose only refuge from their fears and uncertainty is incessant conversation, which reveals to the reader some of the most absurd and contradictory aspects of the Colom-bian armed conflict.*

"Are you awake?"

"Yes."

"I haven't been able to sleep either. The rain soaked my blanket."

"Why is it raining so much when this is the dry season? Why do you think it's been raining so much?"

"I don't know. It's not the rainy season."

"Want a cigarette?"

"Alright."

"Damn. They all got wet."

"It doesn't matter."

"How are we going to smoke them now?"

"It doesn't matter."

"Nothing ever matters to you. I bet it doesn't even bother you that the rain won't let us sleep."

"Rain doesn't bother me."

"Then why haven't you been able to sleep?"

"I've been thinking."

"About what?"

"About tomorrow."

"Are you scared? The lieutenant said they're armed, but I doubt it."

"I've been thinking about why they're sending us there."

"Didn't you hear what the lieutenant said—they refuse to work, they left the plantations and they're looting the villages."

"They're on strike."

"Yeah, but they have no right to be. They also want higher wages."

"They're on strike."

"Exactly. And that's why they're sending us there: to break up the strike."

"That's what I don't like. That's not our job."

"What is not our job?"

"Breaking up strikes."

"Our job is to do whatever is necessary. I'm glad we're going. I've never been to the banana region. And it's better to be on active duty than to be stuck in the barracks—we don't have to pass under review, we don't have to do drills, they can't put you in the brig."

"Yes, they can."

"How can they when we're on active duty?"

"I don't know, but they can."

"In any case, it's better than being in the barracks."

"Yeah, but it's not right."

"What difference does it make if it's right or not? The point is that we're on active duty and not in the barracks."

"It does make a difference."

"So now it does make a difference to you; you're just scared."

"Of course I'm not scared."

"Then what are you so worried about?"

"Because it's a strike, and we should respect it and not get involved."

"They're the ones who should have respect."

"Respect for who?"

"The authorities, us."

"We're not the authorities, we're soldiers. The authorities are the police."

"Yeah, but the police are useless. That's why they're sending us."

"It's just that the police haven't been able to contain them."

"You're scared."

"What the hell! I'm not scared. I just don't like the idea of breaking up a strike. Who knows, maybe the strikers are right."

"They have no right."

"No right to do what?"

"To strike."

"What do you know?"

"The lieutenant said so."

"The lieutenant doesn't know anything."

"You've got a point there."

"He just repeats what the commander says."

"This morning when we were tying up our kit bags, he said, 'Just pack your bedrolls and mats.' And when we were already on our way to the boat, he made us unhitch our bags and remove the bedrolls and mats and then he sent us to the store for the thick blankets. 'You're not riding on the boat; you'll be in the dinghies,' he said. He doesn't know anything."

"Who said they were armed?"

"The lieutenant, when we were falling in for drills. Didn't you hear?"

"No."

"Where do you think they got those weapons?"

"They don't have weapons, just their machetes."

"How do you know?"

"They're day laborers."

"And that explains why they don't have weapons?"

"Yes."

"Help me wring out my blanket, because when we get to the channel there'll be mosquitoes. Grab the other end. And your blanket? You didn't use your blanket?"

"No."

"You're soaked through."

"It doesn't matter."

"What'd you do with your blanket?"

"I wrapped my rifle in it so it wouldn't get wet."

That afternoon they had had to march from the barracks to the port. It was a short walk but their boots were new and big, and the new leather of their cartridge belts and kit bags had still not been broken in by their sweat.

They had to wait at the port for several hours. They were a large contingent and they had to tie up the boats before getting on board. The embarkation was slow. They boarded via the stern and the nails on their boots kept making them slip on the smooth decks. While they waited, they had been ordered to keep their rifles slung across their chests, but the barrels kept hitting against the low crossbeams, and with their canteens and kit bags on their backs they couldn't pass through the corridors on either side of the boiler room. So they had to remove their gear and walk through the boat to the dinghies carrying it in their hands. The embarkation was disorganized and slow. When it was time for the last group to board, they had already been waiting for several hours. They sat on top of the cargo crates in the dinghies, with their rifles between their knees.

Some were scared during the river crossing: there was a strong December wind, and the dinghies lurched violently, out of synch with the ships, tightening and stretching the hawsers that pounded the logs against the gunwales. Those on the sterns of the ships got soaked.

Before entering the channel they could see the city, in its entirety, lit up, on the other side. They had never seen it before.

Each soldier thought he recognized the lights of places he knew. Their initial amazement brought them all together: friends searched for each other over the heads of others craning their necks in search of their friends. One by one they said, "There are the barracks," and they pointed in all directions.

They entered the channel as if into a tunnel. The dinghies were so broad and the ships' beams were so long that they all plowed into the mangrove-covered riverbank, hurtling against each other, constantly having to protect their upright rifles from the collisions.

Everything that was new to them—the incredible burning stream emanating from the smokestacks; the ungainly movements of the boats perfectly obedient to the erratic sounds of the bell; the hillsides that suddenly emerged revealing a ranch, a small bonfire, or the barking of a dog—everything that was new began to look the same, repetitive, familiar. Then they began to slump over their rifles with sleep, against the crates, against the shoulders and backs and hips of the others.

Suddenly, unexpectedly, it started to rain.

I'm hungry. Are we there?"

"Yes."

"Have we been here long?"

"No. We just arrived."

"I fell asleep as soon as we entered the channel. Did you sleep?"

"No."

"A lot of mosquitoes in the channel?"

"No."

"It wasn't true what they said about there being swarms of mosquitoes in the channel. I knew it wasn't true."

"It was true."

"Did it rain all night?"

"Yes."

"What are we waiting for?"

"They're releasing the hawsers."

"Where are we going to have our coffee? I'm hungry."

"I don't know, maybe at the train station."

"Why at the station? Isn't there a garrison here? And anyway we have to hang the blankets out to dry, that is, if the sun comes out today. You need to let your uniform dry."

"I don't think we're going to have time to hang anything out to dry."

"Have the others already disembarked?"

"No, we're the first."

"Get up; they're going ashore. I'm numb. Damn rain."

"We still have time."

"But the group at the prow are already getting off. We should wait until the sun comes up; I can't see a thing."

"They're in a hurry."

"What for? Oh, yeah, to break up the strike."

"We might not be able to break up the strike."

"Of course we will."

"Maybe we won't."

"So you think they're armed, too?"

"No, they're not armed."

"It's going to be a cinch."

"Who knows?"

"Get up, it's our turn."

"You're in a hurry too."

"No, I don't give a damn about the strike, it's just that I'm numb and hungry."

"Then let's get going."

"No, wait. I'm going to take a piss here and soak the place good."

When the dinghies bumped against the muddy slope and then went still, those who were asleep began to wake up. The sun still hadn't come up. They woke up slowly: first, their arms and legs and bodies recognized the proximity of other arms, legs, and bodies; then they gripped and released their rifles to remind themselves of their shape and bulk; lastly, their eyes began to distinguish points of reference in the darkness.

The searchlights from the boats meticulously traveled along the dinghies. Like an affront. The light struck their faces with a burning, open-handed slap. Some shielded their faces with their free arms, others turned around only to find the lights gliding along their wet caps and the damp backs of their necks. Now everyone was awake.

The disembarkation was less slow and less disorderly. They were eager to move and to get ashore. They didn't mind having to walk through the murky water that lay between the prows of the dinghies and the riverbank. They were eager to move. They submerged themselves into the water and the riverbed gave way under the double weight of their bodies and their gear. Their legs sank into the mud with a fetid squish. But they disembarked rapidly and almost rushed through the stretch of water that led to the steep riverbank, which they climbed steadying themselves on the butts of their rifles.

The only thing I had left that wasn't wet were my boots. Now I'm soaked to the bone. I'm going to take them off."

"We still have to walk to the station."

"Just to empty them—they're full of water."

"It's a long walk to the station."

"How far is it?"

"About a league."

"Then where the hell are we going to have our coffee?"

"At the station."

"We should set up camp here and have our coffee. Then we can go wherever they want."

"We have to be at the station when the train arrives."

"The train? What train?"

"The one that's going to take us to the banana region."

"Oh, yeah, that's right. You told me last night, but I forgot. It's impossible to think straight with this hunger. When does the train leave?"

"I don't think it's running today. The railway men are on strike."

"Them, too? And what do they have to do with the day laborers?"

"Nothing."

"They've just jumped on the bandwagon, then."

"No. They don't have any job security either. They stopped running the trains to help out the strikers."

"Good for them."

"Who's going to operate the train, then?"

"I don't know. They'll send a detachment to look for them and make them work."

"Why 'good for them'?"

"Because otherwise how are we going to get to the towns to break up the strike?"

"We'd be better off not going to the towns. We'd be better off not having to kill anybody."

"We're better off not being in the barracks, like now. Look how soft my boots have gotten with the water. I almost don't feel them anymore. The problem is that once the sun comes up, they'll get as hard as wood again."

"The engineers should hide."

"What?"

"Nothing."

"Feel this boot: see how soft it is? Wet yours so they'll soften up too."

"They're wet."

"Take them off and wash them like I did: you sink them in the water and then take them out, dip in, take out, dip in, take out. They'll get soft and clean. Go ahead, you'll see."

"There's no time; here comes the sergeant giving the order to fall in."

"What are we going to fall in for?"

"To count off."

"What, are they afraid some recruit fell into the river or something? They shouldn't have sent recruits."

"No, not that they've fallen into the river, that they've run away."

"Run away? Why would anyone run away from being out of the barracks? What's the point? You run away when you're cooped up inside."

"That someone's deserted, I think."

"You mean deserter, that there's a deserter."

"Yeah, whatever."

"But there's no such thing as a deserter when you're on a mission. Deserters are when you're at war and right now we're not at war, we're on a mission."

"Alright, that someone's escaped, then, that someone has escaped because he doesn't want to take part in this."

"One hundred eighty-four."

"One hundred eighty-five."

Do you want some more coffee?"

"I'm not hungry."

"After making us wait all this time, all they give us is coffee. I'm still hungry."

"You can have mine."

"You're sure you don't want it?"

"Yeah. Give me a cigarette."

"They're not dry yet."

"It doesn't matter, give me one anyway."

"You like chewing it?"

"It distracts me."

"Nothing can distract my stomach now. It's growling. Chewing tobacco gets rid of your hunger?"

"Yes."

"I'm going to chew some to see if it works for me. Where'd you learn this?"

"A long time ago, in my town."

"To get rid of your hunger then, too?"

"Yes. There was never enough food."

"The same shit as in the barracks."

"There's not enough food here because the sergeants steal the money. In my house, it was because there wasn't any money."

"They steal the money and the food. I've bought food from the supplier, and I've heard that the sergeant's wife has a store where she sells all the stuff her husband has taken from the depot."

"Whoever got us this coffee must have stolen a ton; they didn't even give us rolls."

"I'm going to ask the women who brought the pots."

"What for? If the sergeant finds out that you've gone around asking questions, he'll put you in the brig."

"They can't put me in the brig here, we're not in the barracks."

"They'll discipline you, then."

"They should report it to the commander."

"The commander steals, too."

"No, I don't think so."

"He's the worst thief of them all."

"Okay, everyone steals. But the sergeant is the worst because he steals from us: he pockets the money for our food and makes us go hungry. If the commander steals, he steals from the government, and that doesn't matter."

"It matters more, because that means he's stealing from his country."

"The country is not the government; the country is the gold, blue, and red. Stealing from the government is not stealing; everyone knows that. Let's go over there and join those guys. You coming?"

"No, I have to clean my rifle; it got mud in it when we disembarked."

"Mine sunk into the mud too, but I'm not going to clean it now."

"I am. I'm not going to go around with a rusty rifle."

You know what? There are women in this town."

"Who says?"

"No one. I saw them."

"Where?"

"At that house on the corner, in front of the one that says hotel. I went looking for the women who made the coffee to see if there was anything to eat, and the window was open and I saw the women."

"They're probably not that kind."

"Yes, they are. They're wearing long dresses and their faces are all made up. And the room is decorated with streamers, like for a party. Of course they are. Do you think we'll have time to check them out?"

"I don't know."

"The only thing is they don't look French; they look like they're from here."

"Then they're not those kinds of girls."

"That train's never going to come."

"I hope it doesn't."

"Why?"

"That way we won't have to go."

"And what if they make us walk? I hope it comes."

"They won't make us walk."

"How do you know?"

"The towns are far away."

"You've been to the towns?"

"No."

"Which town are we going to?"

"I don't know. I guess to all of them."

"All of them are on strike?"

"The banana region is on strike."

"And all of the towns around here are part of the banana region?"

"Yes."

"How many towns are there?"

"I don't know."

"A lot?"

"Yes, a lot. You sure ask a lot of questions."

"You don't like me asking you questions?"

"I could care less."

"I hope there are a lot of towns. That way it'll take us a long time to break up the strike, and we won't have to go back to the barracks. It's so boring waiting here. What's happened to that train?"

"I guess they haven't been able to find the engineers. Or maybe they haven't been able to make them come."

"We would have kicked their asses all the way here. I bet they sent some of those idiots to get them. We would have had them here long ago."

"You think?"

"Sure; I would have kicked their asses all the way here. I don't think those guys are armed."

"We have no right to beat them up. We can't make them come if they don't want to."

"Of course we have the right; that's what we're here for."

"They're on strike."

"I know, but it doesn't make any difference."

"It does too."

"Fine. What a drag, that damn train not coming."

You think they'll let us go and check out those women?"

"I don't know. I doubt it."

"But what if the train doesn't come? They'll have to take us somewhere; we can't stay here in the station all day."

"If the train doesn't come today, they'll make us spend the night in the garrison."

"There's a garrison in this town?"

"Yes."

"But there aren't any soldiers."

"Just a few."

"Where's the garrison?"

"In the plaza, in front of the church."

"You've been in this town before?"

"No."

"Then how do you know?"

"Garrisons and churches are always next to each other, they're always in the plazas."

"If we end up spending the night here, I'm sneaking out; I really want to go check out those women."

I've never been on a train before. You?"

"Yeah, I have."

"Lots of times?"

"Yes."

"Do you like riding in trains?"

"I prefer to watch them go by."

"I've seen them go by, but I've never ridden in one."

"We lived near a train stop for a while."

"Like this one?"

"No, this is a station. Over there it didn't always stop, only when there were passengers. We used to go there every day to sell figs. When the train didn't stop we'd eat all the figs ourselves."

"So you didn't want it to stop."

"No, we did, because then we could sell a few figs and we'd be able to drink coffee for two or three mornings."

"I like figs more than coffee. You?"

"I don't know. It's been so long since I've eaten figs and there were so many mornings when we didn't have any coffee to drink that I've forgotten the difference."

"What were the figs like?"

"Big and purple with lots of tiny little balls inside."

"What were the trains like?"

"Long and cheerful, and when they didn't stop the people waved from the cars. That was the best."

"The only train I've ever seen is the one in Puerto Colombia, but it's small and I've never seen it move. When it stops, no one waves, right?"

"No, they don't wave. They just look."

This town is ugly."

"All towns are alike."

"But this one's uglier. I had never seen walls covered with salt before. They don't have to buy salt here, all they have to do is scrape it off the walls."

"You don't eat that kind of salt."

"Why not?"

"I don't know, but you don't eat it."

"They don't make them work at all at this garrison. Everything's rusted and full of salt."

"Yeah, that's true."

"Did you notice that no one came out to look at us when we arrived? Not even the children."

"It's because they know why we're here. They already hate us."

"What do they hate us for? It's not our fault."

"Who knows?"

"It's the strikers' fault."

"Not the strikers' fault, the banana company's."

"Fine, but it's not our fault."

"Who knows?"

"Did you see the house next door? It's big, it takes up a whole block: we can escape through there tonight. And it's all closed up. You think there are people inside?"

"Sure there are."

"It doesn't matter. The patio is right next to ours and the wall is low; we can go through there."

"Not me, I don't want to go."

"I do; I'm taking off tonight."

They walked from the station to the town garrison. With their rifles slung across their chests and their kit bags over their right shoulders, they walked along streets covered with hot, salty mud and through puddles full of salt and fresh water. Some removed their boots, which had dried, and stood in the puddles splashing the thick water. They walked slowly, taking their time, watching uncomprehendingly the closed doors and windows on either side of the street.

They had spent the whole day at the station: the first soldiers to arrive sat on the long, wooden benches, and the others scattered about the floor, leaning against the gray steel columns, squatting all along the platform. Some had fallen asleep; others had stared for a long time at the empty tracks merging in the distance until they disappeared at some blurred point at the base of the mountain. Everyone was annoyed. They got tired of watching the closed, dead town, which began in front of the station. After a few hours, they didn't care anymore. They gathered around what they knew: their rifles and their kit bags and their friends, and then they didn't expect anything anymore.

The distance between the station and the garrison was short, and they walked it in silence, along streets and alongside houses, also silent.

The garrison was dirty and nearly uninhabited. They walked through the main patio surrounded by arches and doors, paved with red, fresh bricks. They started to fall in: they dropped their kit bags onto one side and placed their rifles on the ground on the other side; they stepped forward and back, with short, consecutive steps, lining up; then, motionless, with their feet apart, they counted off. When they were given the order to fall out, they already knew which doors they were headed for and on which cot they were going to throw their helmets and hang their blankets. They were themselves again. They had regained their routine.

You're not going to sleep?"

"I'm not sleepy."

"Then come with me."

"No."

"Do you have any money on you?"

"Yeah, two pesos."

"Will you lend me one?"

"Alright."

"You're sure you don't want to come? Let's get out of here; they've already sounded the all quiet."

"I don't feel like it."

"Just come and take a look. I swear they don't look like French girls."

"They're probably not that kind."

"Yes they are, I saw them. Come on, maybe these ones will let us take our pants off."

"I don't want to, I don't want to, I don't want to."

"Alright already, don't get mad."

"I'm not mad, I just don't want to go."

"I'll be right back. Okay?"

"Okay."

"Are you going to stay up all night again?"

"No. I'm going to sleep now."

"Keep an eye on my things, will you?"

"Yeah. Be careful, they might be out patrolling."

"Don't worry, they won't catch me. I wish we could go together."

"I don't feel like it. If you're going to go, then get going."

"I'll be right back."
"Okay."

The train was long, unruly, and instead of cheerful like other trains, it was slow and awkward, and its cars, exposed to the elements, banged against each other unnecessarily. The engine stopped in front of the station. Those who were riding in the engineer's cabin and on the roof of the second car did not get off. They remained seated, with their rifles between their legs, watching the engineers.

When the order was given to fall in, those who were scattered all over the train ran with practiced haste and gathered in front of the engine. The group gradually formed into a straight line, stretching out, shrinking, until they were compact and even. When the noise of boots, rifles, and kit bags had subsided, they started to count off. There were very few of them. The first turned to his right, raised his rifle, and began to walk. He walked through the station and into the town. The rest followed him with the same movements. The last two turned to their left, laid their rifles horizontally across their cartridge belts, and began their incessant back and forth patrolling of the platform.

Then they heard the whistle: short, sharp, cold—like a knife, like a sign.

The column halted, running into each other briefly. Some turned their heads, mechanically, indifferently, unfazed. Then, without having understood, they continued walking.

The bugler ran across the still dark patio and climbed onto the dais. The clean, precise, familiar sound filled the garrison.

In the long-silent sleeping quarters, the rusty steel of the beds began to creak and for a moment the sounds of bodies, boots, canteens, and rifles, and above all the uncertain din of urgency, obscured the sound of the bugle.

They fell in, in columns of four, with their backs to the dais where the bugle continued sounding, urging. Then the bugle fell silent and the vast space all of the sounds had inhabited slowly filled with the sunlight that began to fall onto the patio.

They did not count off.

With precise steps marking the rhythm of the voice commanding them in formation, their rifles slung on their shoulders and their kit bags tight against their backs, they left the garrison. They marched along the same streets, with their eyes fixed on the back of the neck of the soldier marching in front of them, without turning their heads to look at the dark openings in the doorways or the open windows. With sure steps they marched through the puddles and on the salty mud. The water of the puddles jumped now under the weight of the bodies, the double weight of metal and leather. The mud leapt, glistening, at each thud of their boots. They marched in columns of four, and one of three, to the station.

They were not death yet, but they carried death on their fingertips. They marched with death glued to their legs. Death struck their buttocks at each juncture. Death weighed on their left clavicles, a death of metal and wood that they had dutifully cleaned.

Those who had remained in the station gathered on the other side of the street, in front of the hotel. They were scared at first. There were seven of them, but the men did not show signs of hostility, only curiosity. There they were, on the other side of the street, with their rifles still laying across their cartridge belts, merely watching, not really understanding what was going on, not even trying to understand, simply watching as the men started to arrive in groups, emerging from all of the streets and all of the houses that had appeared deserted and empty. And when the people had gathered in the station and were already a throng, they boarded the train cars, the engine. And when there was no room left in the cars, they climbed up onto the roofs of the cars and the roof of the engine. They occupied the train, filling it with their clean clothing, small yellow straw hats, and machetes still inside their well-worn sheaths. They covered the train, squeezed against each other in the open cars and on the roofs of the closed cars, hanging from the steps to the cars and from the footboard of the engine. And they remained on the train, in silence, with determination and in peace.

I looked all over for you and I couldn't find you. I was scared; I got scared when I heard so many shots. Why did they kill them? They were unarmed. You were right—they were unarmed. And now what are we going to do? I have to go back, I want to see her by day; I want to see what she looks like during the day. Do you think we're going to go back to the barracks? They can't leave us here with all of these corpses. You know what? I didn't go to see those women. I didn't need to. In the house next door, remember, the one that's closed up, there are people. She must live there because she was on the patio, alone on the patio. I didn't get a good look at her face. And she didn't speak. Afterwards, a little while after, she started to cry, not screaming, just slowly—you could hardly tell that she was crying. I don't get it; I don't get anything. You have to come back with me; you have to explain it to me. She didn't touch me, she didn't hold me, she didn't even lift her arms. With her eyes open, she just let me do it. I didn't force her. You're not going to believe me, but I didn't force her. She let me. I didn't get a good look at her, but she's almost my height and she smelled like ylang-ylang flowers. At first she smelled like ylang-ylang; then she smelled like blood. Look at my fingers—it's as if I had cut myself. That's why I took so long, because she left right after; she went into the house, and I stayed on the patio looking at the dark corridor. I stayed there all night staring at the dark corridor. I stayed all night looking at the corridor without knowing what to do. Now I know that I was already scared before hearing the gunshots."

"They were sitting on the roof of the train car. I went up to them. One of them lowered his arms. I thought he might jump off. When I raised my rifle, the barrel nearly touched his stomach. I don't know if he was going to jump, but I saw him lower his arms. With the barrel almost touching his stomach, I pulled the trigger. He was suspended in the air like a kite. Hanging from the end of my rifle. Suddenly he fell. I heard the shot. He fell off the end of my rifle and onto my face, onto my shoulders, onto my boots. And then the stench. He smelled like shit. And the smell has covered me like a thick, sticky blanket. I've smelled the barrel of my gun, I've smelled the sleeves and front of my shirt, I've smelled my pants and my boots. And it's not blood; I'm not covered with blood, I'm covered with shit."

"It's not your fault; you had to do it."

"No, I didn't have to do it."

"They gave the order to shoot."

"Yes."

"They gave the order to shoot and you had to do it."

"I didn't have to kill him; I didn't have to kill a man I didn't know."

"They gave the order, everyone fired; you had to fire too. Don't worry so much."

"I could have raised my rifle, just raised it but without shooting."

"Yes, that's true."

"But I didn't."

"It was out of habit—they gave the order and you fired. It's not your fault."

"Whose fault is it then?"

"I don't know—it's the habit of obeying orders."

"It has to be someone's fault."

"Not someone. Everyone. It's everyone's fault."

"Damn it, damn it."

"Don't worry about it. Do you think she'll remember me?"

"In this town they will remember all of us. In this town they will always remember; we are the ones who will forget."

"Yeah, you're right; they will remember."

My Father Was Blue

Nicolás Suescún

Red or blue?

In Colombia, the color red has traditionally been associated with liberals and the Colombian Liberal Party, which in political jargon is—or was—progressive, freethinking, and left of center. Associated with those right of center, blue has been the color of the conservatives and the Conservative Party of Colombia, of the status quo, of centralized regimes intent on "law and order," regimes often allied with the Catholic Church hierarchy. The time came, however, when this nomenclature ceased in large part to be a matter of ideology or political convictions. One was born blue or red by tradition, family, or inertia. One lived as blue or red with many of the consequences and in some areas with its horrific implications. And sometimes one was even buried blue or red; some Colombian towns particularly ravaged by the violence went so far as to have separate cemeteries for liberals and conservatives.

Nicolás Suescún's story reveals a critical moment in this division when a group of hot-headed troublemakers from one of the two political parties appears in a town like any other and demands that the mayor immediately proclaim himself blue or red.

My father was blue. The town mayor. One day a group of bandits that had spread panic throughout the region came to our town on sweaty and hungry horses. In the plaza they swept up enormous pillars of dust. My father came out to meet them.

They spoke first. "Are you blue, or red?"

"I'm the mayor," he said.

"That was not the question. What we want to know is if you are our friend or our enemy."

"Why don't we make a deal. I can help you."

"We don't need your help. We have asked you a question. Give us an answer or consider yourself dead."

"I'm red," he said finally, and they riddled him with bullets.

"That'll teach you, fucking red."

And since he did not die right away, they undressed him, tied him to a tree, and cut off his penis with a machete.

He said, "No, no, this is all a mistake; I'm blue, blue."

"So now you change sides," they said. "We would have killed you anyway. We don't like mayors."

Years later, I joined them to avenge his death. I don't like to kill old men. I prefer women and children.

The Day We Buried Our Weapons

Plinio Apuleyo Mendoza

In the so-called period of violence in Colombia (roughly speaking, an undeclared civil war between Liberals and Conservatives and those acting at their behest), which lasted for close to thirty years, the intensity of the armed conflict and the frequency and ferocity of the battles, ambushes, and murders—or summary death sentences, from the opposing point of view—have varied a great deal depending on who happened to be in office, the party in power, the veiled participation of other foreign actors, and the truces and cease-fires agreed to, among many other factors. Unfortunately, one of the few things that can be counted on in the recent history of the country is that sooner or later the cycle of violence will repeat itself and after a while, the opposing parties will fight each other again.

Such is the premise of this story. In this case, the setting is the eastern plains. The protagonists have pursued the conflict rather philosophically, and after coming under a truce they prepare to carry out another of the rituals of armed conflict: hiding their weapons in preparation for the next cycle of hostilities.

Four years of fighting, yes sir; four years of exchanging fire with the government troops. If it weren't for the deaths and for death, which every so often came grazing the brims of our hats, you could say that it was all one big party. Get used to it, I would say to my men; you're going to die, you are as good as dead, so don't be surprised when the

31

day comes. At first there weren't many of us and we were barefoot, poorly armed with revolvers and shotguns, slinking through ghostly trails, far from the sugarcane mills and the main roads where the troops were. We hung our hammocks from the struts of abandoned ranch houses, and so we wouldn't be discovered, we had to behead all the roosters and hang the mountain dogs. Then, the party started.

The government sent more troops, and the troops came setting fire to the ranches along the way, and within one long year we were no longer dozens but thousands. The eastern plains, from Arauca to San Martín, were boiling over with rebels. The government troops couldn't hack it even with all of their planes and bombs.

What years! I still remember getting up at dawn with the guerillas, the bitter coffee and the breeze blowing across the scrubland as the last stars faded. I remember the bonfires, the nightly conversations from hammock to hammock. The closer they got to us, the more we felt like brothers, like *compas*. I don't know why we started calling each other *compa*. See you later, *compa!* What's up, *compa?* That's how we always talked to each other. What a time that was! To think that we were so close to victory. To think that they traded in our revolution for a coup, poor rebels.

I remember, like it was yesterday, the day we buried our weapons. The night before, instead of bombs, the military planes had hurled bunches of newspapers and a flood of pamphlets onto the camp. The newspapers spoke of the end of the dictatorship, of peace, of amnesty, of the peaceful surrender of guerillas all over the plains. And it was true, there were the photos of Guadalupe, de Aluma, the Galindo brothers, and Miguel Suarez, in front of their columns of rebels in formation, handing their weapons over to the military. Peace. Amnesty. Two words and everyone let down their guard. And as for us, what could we do? Ours was the guerilla commando unit that fought closest to the Venezuelan border; it was the furthest, the most remote. For a moment we thought we could keep fighting. But no chance; they would have crushed us. We had no doubt when the messengers came saying there was celebration in the towns, flags and the national anthem everywhere, and the people, our people, exchanging their weapons for bags of salt and sugar, sometimes for less, for a speech and a little bouquet of flowers from the schoolgirls. So we decided to end the party our own way. We decided to bury our weapons and disband once and for all.

I remember that we got up at dawn to take down the hammocks and pack our gear. Before saddling up the horses, I ordered the branches from the bonfires to be crushed and for dirt to be scattered over the ashes so as not to leave any trace of our camp. When the time came to disperse, I called together my men. They were silent, reticent. We had been doing the same thing for so long. . . . Many of them had come to the plains at the very beginning, four years before, for no other purpose than to save their skins, hungry, scared, flea-ridden. To survive, they had had to get smart—those who didn't, died. They had learned to move together in packs all over the plains. They had learned to move out at a moment's notice, to slink through the mountains like Indians and make traps to hunt the government troops like venison. And now here I was with the sad story: the party's over, hand over your weapons, and go your own way, with only your horse for company and a change of clothes. They had every reason to be suspicious. As a last reminder of who they had been, I decided to leave them with one last order.

"Take off all of your military gear," I said. "No helmets, shakos, or red bandanas around your necks. No camouflage."

They were noticeably disgruntled when I ordered Puntería, my second in command, to collect their arms. They looked at each other nervously. One, speaking for all of them, dared to ask what I planned on doing with the guns. I saw right then and there that they had been holding back the question; their eyes gave them away.

"Bury them," I said.

"Where?" they asked.

"In a safe place. Call it a military secret."

"Buried treasure for the rebels," said Puntería, still gathering the rifles and placing them on a piece of oilcloth. But no one laughed. They kept looking at me, each seeing their own doubts reflected in the others' faces.

"That's it, the rebels' buried treasure," I said. "And it won't be long before the guns are back in your hands. Think of this as just a breather."

"But the savannah is big, Colonel," one said.

"No matter: there's no shot in Arauca that can't be heard in San Martín. It's small enough for us to find each other."

I remember that there was a silence, and during that silence we heard somewhere, near the river, the squawking of guacharacas.

"Let's go," I announced, to put an end to the discussion. "The guerilla way, no good-byes."

They started breaking out of the circle, throwing their saddlebags over their shoulders, reluctantly and slowly, as if in pain. And that's how it all ended.

Puntería helped me carry the weapons to the riverbank. Puntería was one of our best men: small and sly like a cat, with cat-like yellow eyes, too, which you could barely see under his felt hat. He and his older brothers had descended the mountains to the plains when the police had arrived in northern Boyacá razing all the liberal villages in their path; he was the only one of his four brothers to have survived.

"The fact is that no one wants to go back to their ranches and villages just to champ at the bit again," he said. "They'll disband, but they don't know where to go."

Now that the war was over, Puntería felt drawn to the jungle; he wanted to go to Vichada. I wasn't sure myself where I'd end up hanging my hammock.

"Maybe I'll go to Venezuela," I said. "Venezuela's right there, on the other side of the river."

The boat was ready, with its outboard motor installed and the prow run ashore. Manolo Sandoval was waiting for us with a barrel, three shovels, and a large sack full of lime. Everything was ready for the burial. When we had finished bringing over all of the weapons, we counted ten rifles, one FA assault rifle, and a Thompson machine gun, all of which we wrapped in oilcloth and placed in the boat.

We found a good place downriver. I'd still be able to recognize it by the enormous fig tree rising from a promontory on the dead leaves of the riverbank. Facing the fig tree, on the other side of the

river, there's a yellow ravine. I carefully examined the stubble.
Then, we had to clear a path to the foot of the tree. Puntería, on his
hands and knees, picked up a clod of dirt and inspected it. He said
that it was dry soil and well elevated; there was no danger of flood-
ing. Manolo had been listening to the screeching of the macaws in
the hills.

"This place is bewitched," he said.

We dug at a distance of five feet from the fig tree so the hole would
be out of reach of its roots. We worked for an hour. First we cleared
the plot with a machete; then we started digging like gravediggers—
pushing in the shovels with our boots because the earth seemed to
have been hardened by the summer—until the hole was five feet
deep. Then we put the barrel that had been prepared with tree gum
inside, poured in the lime, and placed the weapons on top. Lastly,
we carefully put the top on the barrel and covered it with fifteen
inches of well-packed soil.

When we finished, more than two inches of sun had left the
savannah. I remember that Manolo, wiping the sweat off his chest
with his shirt, which he had hung from a tree branch, said, "Colonel, it's time to say an Our Father for this revolution that has just
died on you." Manolo was always joking around. He was a rich kid,
from a good family, who had ended up joining the guerrillas for a
lark when we occupied his old Aunt Victoria Amaya's ranch. I think
he had had a falling out with his girlfriend. He wrote poetry. . . . For
him, the guerrilla war had been one big party. And to keep the party
going, he came with me to Venezuela.

We continued downriver all day. I can still see the riverbanks
and the sun reflecting in the water. It was summer. The fields of the
savannah were yellow. We sometimes passed ferryboats heading up
the Meta River with their usual cargo of salt and gasoline drums.
The boaters greeted us as they passed. I eventually fell asleep, lulled
by the sound of the motor. I remember I had a strange dream. I
dreamed that the military had captured my men, that they were in a
ferryboat with their hands tied behind their backs, and that as we
passed them, they said, "Colonel, they give us cups of coffee, and
then they break our bones."

When I woke up, the riverbanks had receded. The sun, on the Colombian side, was red; the horizon looked like it was on fire. On the Venezuelan side, there were immense boulders lit up like coals. The water crashed against them, forming waves. The wind was blowing very hard. From the smell I knew that we had arrived at the Orinoco. Puntería, sitting next to the tiller, confirmed it at the top of his lungs. Manolo, waking up, pointed at a flock of parrots flying toward Colombia.

"Say good-bye to your countrymen," he said.

We finally caught the first glimpses of the lights from the electric plant in Port Paez, on the Venezuelan side, glittering between rocks and zinc roofs. It was the largest town I had seen in a long time, at least since the war had begun. I thought that for the first time in a long while I'd be able to take a hot bath, eat three meals a day. Wow, and drink an ice-cold glass of water! This is what one thinks about after having been on the run for so long.

We tied up on a sandbank two hundred yards from the first houses.

Puntería didn't want to stay with us in Venezuela. He let us off at the sandbank and then headed toward the other side of the river. I can still see his white shirt and his felt hat disappearing into the darkness of the river. I don't think he ever made it to Vichada. He was killed in a cantina in Villavicencio. Shot dead. Like Guadalupe and Suarez. The army made them all pay, one by one. It's so easy to break a lone branch. . . . Those who returned to the hills, having realized they had been tricked before it was too late, had to live the rest of their lives labeled as bandits. And with the label as their epitaph, so they died. But that's another story.

I stayed in Venezuela. Manolo, who wasn't the exile type, returned home. He regained his bearings when his father died. Today he's a rich cattle rancher, fat, with a son studying at the Naval Academy: not a trace of the guerrilla he had once been. As for me, well . . . the years flew by without me even noticing. I did a little of everything, I worked in Caracas, in Puerto Cabello; I even went to Guayana looking for diamonds.

The Day We Buried Our Weapons

Every once in a while, behind a shop counter, in a gas station, or driving a truck, I come across one of my guerrillas, one of the old-timers. We have a beer and talk about the revolution, and we drink to the other one, for the one that is to come. But who am I kidding? Now that there are so many boys talking about Fidel and Che and wanting to take to the mountains, I realize that it is too late for us. There's nothing for us to do; we missed the train. It's whistling far away. Look, my hair's gone gray, my belly's bulging. Last month I had to buy glasses so I could read the newspaper. And here I am in this town, selling liquor like any old shopkeeper. At night, when it's too hot to sleep in my room, I take a stool out onto the street. I think about a lot of things. Jeez, I sometimes wonder, what happened to you, Emilio Santos? How'd you manage to get so old so fast?

From the war, what keeps coming back to me, most vividly, is the day we buried our weapons. And the worst of it is that our weapons are still there, waiting for us. At the foot of the fig tree. I'd like to find the boys who have the same itch now that I had. I'd like to take them over there, to the Meta River, where so many years ago we buried the treasure. Ten rifles, an FA assault rifle, and a Thompson machine gun are a good start. I'd like to say to them, "There you have it; go after it, boys, go after it. It's your party now."

Prelude

Hernando Téllez

On April 9, 1948, on a street in downtown Bogotá, attorney Jorge Eliécer Gaitán, liberal party candidate for the presidency, was assassinated. Although the position he took along the ideological spectrum was rather ambivalent, his firebrand populist rhetoric and modest middle-class origins had made him a hero amongst the workers, peasants, and dispossessed masses. His assassination unleashed in the capital an explosion of violence, mostly spontaneous, which soon spread throughout most of the country: The Bogotazo, as that day is known, is considered the starting point of the era known as "The Violence."

In this story Hernando Téllez chooses an anonymous and incidental protagonist to give voice to a brief and terrible account of that day, as if of a portent of what was to come.

First there was a scream. Then thousands of screams. Then turmoil. Then the revolution. I was given a machete, big and brand new. As I turned it over and over against the pale light, the blade sparkled.

"Hey there, young man, here's your weapon."

"Thank you."

The machete was heavy. My whole hand could fit comfortably on the wooden handle, gripping it the way it's supposed to be: my fist closed around it, with the piece of wood in my palm.

"But what do I do with the machete?"

The group was leaving. And the man who had given it to me was already up the street, at the head of his friends.

"Mister, what do I do with the machete?" I asked desperately.

Neither he nor the others heard me. Everyone was screaming, possessed, violent. My question dissipated in the air. Superimposed on everyone's faces was the face of the revolution: rage and fear, red and white. The revolution had caught me out on the street, as I was standing in front of a bakery shop window on the main avenue. Only one minute before, my hands were empty—in a pose of helplessness, of someone who has no job, of someone who is a little hungry—imagining the possibility of one day being able to go into that shop and eat, meticulously, one after the other, all of the pastries in the window. One minute later the revolution was presenting me with a gift in the form of a machete. But what for? I didn't know.

It must have been in the south where the revolution had erupted like a gigantic bloom of flames, because in that direction, and despite the distance, a reddish glow managed to penetrate the leaden sky, gilding it in parts, like a copper coin. Faraway, indistinct gunshots were carried toward us by the wind. With the machete in my hands I began to think about the revolution. Who was it against? Who was it for?

"Excuse me, sir, what's happened?"

The old man looked at my hands and, turning pale, broke into a comical run. But more and more people continued to march past. The street was a river of water that dragged along, in its turn, a river of people.

"Miss," I said, grasping a girl's arm, "can you tell me what has happened?"

She anxiously released herself from my grip and answered in a trembling voice, "I don't know, I don't know, don't stop me, please. I'm going home."

"But, what's happened?"

She had already gone away. The machete was, of course, an impediment. With it in my hands, I must have looked like one of the real revolutionaries. But I wasn't a revolutionary. I was a poor wretch who had wandered around with nowhere to go, with ten cents in his pocket, and who had stopped to look in a shop window. I looked for my reflection in the glass: the machete hung parallel to my tattered pants, on the right side. The ensemble didn't look half bad. The machete gave me a certain air of dignity. But what was I going to do with the machete? The revolution can't be mistaken, I thought; if they're giving out machetes there must be something to slash, there must be something to defend, and someone must have to be killed. I laughed and turned around. A merciless rain had begun to fall.

Another raging group walked by and several of them looked at me, first with hostility, then with hate, but when they saw the weapon dangling from my right hand, they smiled ominously. And one of them, facing me, roared, "Viva the revolution!"

I responded automatically, "Viva!" And I suddenly found myself brandishing the weapon, possessed by an incredible rage.

But they walked on. The rain's momentum intensified and, under the rain, the people continued running and screaming, crazed, scared, some irate, others defiant, many hesitant, all already marked by the strange stamp of that great and terrible thing that had been born, suddenly, somewhere in the city.

I took refuge in the doorway to the shop and only then did I realize that it was closed. The time left no room for doubt: eight minutes past two in the afternoon. The owners would be arriving soon. But would they? Who knows! I emerged from the doorway. The rain soaked my clothing and poured off the brim of my hat, and I felt its sogginess rising through the soles of my shoes to my holed socks and to my feet. A truck, full of men who were holding a flag, sped by. And the fan of mud thrown by its tires hit me right in the face. For an instant I was blinded. I tossed the machete onto the ground as I wiped off my face and my clothing.

"Pick up that machete, you wretch!" an authoritative voice commanded behind me. "Pick it up or else I'll teach you to obey," insisted the voice.

I picked it up and turned around to see who was threatening me. His face was not very revealing: ashen skin, bloated cheeks, red eyelids, puffy lips. A man like any other. Like so many who passed by and passed by and ran and threatened and screamed. One of a series, instantly mass-produced by the revolution.

He stared at me. He also had a machete in his hand. The rain poured off of his shoulders; it soaked his clothes, like it soaked mine.

"Viva the revolution!" he yelled, wielding the machete.

I answered, "Viva!"

Without addressing me, he yelled, "Down with the murderers!"

I answered, "Down with them!"

The man was satisfied. He gave me one last look that betrayed his desire to determine my intentions. Then he started walking along the mud that dissolved on the sidewalk.

I turned back to the shop. Behind the large window were the pastries, still intact. And I was again struck by the idea that one day I'd have to gorge myself until I couldn't eat another bite. *It's hunger,* I said to myself. *Of course it's hunger,* I answered myself. Then I raised the machete to break the window. An intense uproar filled the air and I saw people running for cover. I lowered my hand without hitting the glass and barely had time to dive onto the ground, to hit the mud and the water, as another truck passed like lightning, scattering shots.

When I got up, with the machete dripping wet, someone had taken my place in front of the window. It was another man of the same series that for an hour now was being issued into the streets by the revolution. He did not have a weapon. He had a gray, expressionless face. Paltry clothing. An ordinary grimace on his lips. A hat dripping water. Muddy shoes. We stood next to each other, with our backs to the street, looking in the window.

"We can break it," he proposed with absolute coldness. "Hand me the machete."

I was furious. Why the hell should I include this man in an act that was for me alone to do?

"The revolution isn't for stealing," I said, savoring the pleasure of my hypocrisy.

"If you don't break the window, I will," he said somberly.

More gunshots in the distance. The stranger and I remained standing next to each other, but as enemies. The rain continued unabated. The distant glow of the fires intermittently lit up the grimness of the sky. A surging indignation was engulfing me.

I found the man detestable, repugnant like a usurper. The fact was, the revolution had found me there, and there it had left me. That shop window was my territory. Whatever was inside belonged to me.

The man continued looking at me in silence, with mocking eyes.

"And what are you going to break it with?" I said defiantly.

"With my hands."

"If you touch that window I'll kill you," I said, driven by a strange impulse, a secret force that seemed to lie inside me but that I knew was also on the street, in the atmosphere. And I raised my hand with the machete threatening him. The stranger remained unperturbed. I watched him make a fist and launch it into the window, which shattered into pieces, and then I watched how he opened his bloody hand to seize the pastries. But halfway there his hand stopped and his body lurched to one side before collapsing onto the sidewalk with a splash. The blow had fallen precisely on his neck, and it seemed to me that as I struck him, something hard and sonorous was cracking under my hands, exactly like a thin log breaking on my knee.

The mud and water were instantly dyed with blood. The window was finally open. But a feeling of nausea had taken away my hunger and with my hunger my desire to gorge myself until I couldn't eat another bite.

A Christmas Story

Mario Mendoza Zambrano

It's a couple minutes to midnight. The place looks like an abandoned warehouse, a defunct factory, or an old railway station, as the characteristic sound of a freight train can be heard in the distance. A man is tied to a chair. His face is distorted by panic: his skin is yellow, his eyes are bloodshot, a few-days-old beard covers his cheeks, dark circles engulf his eyes, and the corners of his mouth tremble nervously. At his side, a young man in baggy pants and a wool cap acts as his guard with a gun in his hand.

A door opens at the far end of the room and another young man enters. He says quickly, spitting out the words, "Alright, it's time."

"They gave the order?" asks the other.

"Yes, let's get this over with."

The prisoner begs, cries, pleads, offers money to his hired killers. The young men toss a coin to see who will be the executioner. The young guard loses; he checks the bullets in the cartridge case of his gun and places the weapon against the prisoner's temple. When he is about to pull the trigger, he hears fireworks and the place suddenly lights up with multicolored and phantasmagoric lights. The assassin turns his head and his eyes wander, far away, to the other side of the window. He lowers the gun and says, "We'll do it tomorrow. Today is Christmas."

The New Order

Arturo Echeverri Mejía

A "New Order," you say? Whether as a result of rigged elections, infighting in the majority party, or a military uprising that has toppled the presidency—as seems to be the case in Arturo Echeverri Mejía's story—the head of state or political party that has taken over attempts to impose its directives, "supplanting, converting, or annihilating its enemies."

But what seems so urgent in the capital is much less so in remote areas far away from the large urban centers of the Andean region, as is the case with the coastal town of this story in which the inhabitants get along rather well and "belong to one or the other party simply because their parents" did.

Enter into the scene a young captain sent from the interior of the country with an urgent mission, and the mayor of the town, an elderly and benevolent gentleman set in his ways.

With synchronized and firm steps, the captain and Sergeant Gabino walked through the first office, leaving behind the metallic clanking of military equipment, and stopped abruptly in front of the mayor's office. The door was open, but they did not go in. They stood waiting in the doorway, haughty, stiff, emphatic, and as they waited they looked like priests of an exotic religion, mummified in the act of an ancient and transcendental ritual.

The mayor, who was an old man, stood up from behind his desk and went to meet them. Behind his gray hair, behind gray eyebrows that resembled mustaches, a pair of roguish, surprised eyes watched the rigid figure of the captain. He stretched out his hand, a hand that was long like his body, and bony and gaunt like his face. The officer shook it with a rapid and mechanical movement. The mayor smiled, but the captain did not.

"Sergeant," said the captain. "You may leave."

The sergeant saluted, turned on his heels, and left.

"Come in, Captain," said the mayor. "Have a seat."

The officer entered, stopped, and took a look around. He saw a desk, a typewriter, three chairs, a plaster-cast crucifix on a wooden cross, and hanging on the far wall, a color portrait of a man whose harsh features appeared softened by a smile.

"This is comfortable," said the officer.

"Yes, Captain. It's comfortable."

The officer's critical eyes continued in their observation. The mayor fidgeted nervously. He didn't know what to say or what to do. He picked up his eyeglasses and put them down again; he shifted some papers and then knocked over the ink well. The ink had formed a small black pool but had not splashed.

The mayor excused himself because he was a courteous man, and then they both sat down on either side of the desk.

"I'm finally here," said the officer. He removed his helmet and placed it on the desk. Without that fierce, iron, gourd-like helmet, he took on the appearance of a human being.

"It's a very beautiful and pleasant place," said the mayor kindly.

The mayor was a kind old gentleman, and he thought that that mask of gravity and severity did not sit well on the officer's pure, young features, or in his serene and candid eyes. His hands were graceful, long, and delicate. He looked up and, like an old man, thought, *I don't understand.*

"Mayor," said the officer, "I missed you at the port. Did you not receive the official announcement of my arrival?"

"Yes," said the old man, "but it did not indicate the date or time. If I had known when you were coming, I would have gone to meet you. After all, that is one of my duties as mayor . . ."

"I understand," said the officer. He looked over his shoulder and saw the open door. "We need to talk calmly and with discretion, Mayor . . . Do you mind if we close the door?"

The old man stood up, closed the door, and returned. It was strange, that feeling of confinement. He had never felt it before. He had always been available to everyone.

"It's as if I weren't here," said the old man, looking at the door.

The officer looked at it, then looked at the old man and said, "Tell me: how long have you been mayor of this town?"

"Two years, this November."

"So you must know all these people rather well," he said, offering him a cigarette.

"Yes, I know them well. They're the best people in the world." He lit the cigarette. A harsh and prolonged coughing fit erupted with the first exhale of smoke. The officer looked at his bloodshot eyes and dilated veins, and thought, *He's a decrepit old man. He's worn out.*

"Please excuse me," said the mayor as soon as he could. "I rarely smoke. I'm not used to it. Doesn't it ever happen to you?"

"No."

"Are you planning on an extended stay, Captain?"

"Yes," he said dryly. He looked at him with cold eyes and asked, "What were you saying about your people, Mayor?"

"Oh, yes!" he replied. "I was saying, my people are the best in the world. Gabino can tell you. He knows them. And what's more, the jail is always empty; we lost the padlock two months ago, and we haven't needed to replace it. . . ."

"That's very interesting."

"Yes. It's interesting and exemplary."

"And your best people in the world—how do they think?"

"Think? I don't understand, Captain."

"Politically, Mayor. How do they think?"

The old man opened his mouth and stared at him.

"Did I take you by surprise, Mayor?"

"Well, a little," said the old man. "I wasn't expecting that question . . . My people, most of them, belong to the other party . . ."

"I know," the captain replied quickly. "I already knew, but I wanted to ask you. My superiors also wanted to ask you."

"They wanted to ask me?"

"Yes. They wanted to ask you. They also wonder why you, mayor, have done nothing. . . ."

"Nothing?"

"Yes, nothing. These people are against the government. . . ."

"No, not against the government, Captain. My people belong to the other party, but they're not in any way against the government."

"Try to understand, Mayor: either you're with the government, or you're against it. There's no other way."

"Excuse me, Captain, but I don't understand. Our people don't know the first thing about politics. They've never been interested in politics. They belong to one party or the other, simply because their parents belonged to that or the other party. I assure you, Captain, 80 percent of the people in this town don't even know which party currently controls the fate of this nation."

"Please, Mayor," the officer said firmly. "Try to understand."

"I'll try, Captain. . . ."

"Don't try!" exclaimed the officer. "Understand!"

"Alright," he said, and his gleaming eyes looked fiercely through his bushy eyebrows. His gaunt, old face had acquired a pallid hue.

"We, the military, do not give advice. We give orders," he said calmly, dispassionately, stroking the handle of his gun, implication and essence of all persuasion.

"Now I understand," said the old man deviously and with fire coursing through his blood.

"Let's not play games, Mayor, and get that look off your face," said the officer, slowly and softly. "My job is to make people understand."

He stretched out his hand offering another cigarette. The butt of the previous one was still burning. The old man shook his head.

"Thank you, Captain," he said. "I don't smoke anymore. No offense. It makes me cough."

The officer lit his cigarette and put out the match, shaking it in the air as he reflected. He asked, "Did you draw up the lists we asked for of the people belonging to our party, Mayor?"

"Yes," said the old man. He picked up his glasses, put them on, and took some papers out of a drawer. "There are fourteen of them. Here is the list, Captain."

The officer looked it over rapidly. "Only fourteen?" he asked.

"Yes," said the old man. "You'll see my name there, too."

He leaned forward and pointed to his name with his index finger.

"And how many belong to the opposition party?"

"A few thousand, Captain."

The officer's large, black, expressionless eyes looked at the old man's glasses.

"You must know all of them, isn't that right, Mayor?"

"All of them," said the old man. "This is a village where we all live as brothers."

"There is currently in effect," said the officer, "a 'new order.' Are you aware of this, Mayor?"

"Yes," said the old man.

"And the fourteen people on the list, are they aware of this too?"

The old man hesitated. Then, peering above the rim of his glasses, he said, "Actually, we've had a hard time understanding what this 'new order' is exactly. I was ordered to fill all of the local government posts with people from our party, and I did. They all work for the government now. . . ."

"How many posts does this town have?"

"Seventeen, Captain."

"So," said the captain, "there are three vacancies. . . ."

"No, Captain. At first I was going to ask three capable individuals from the other party, but my superiors in the city were opposed to it. They later ordered me to give two of the posts to people from our party. . . ."

"And did you?"

"Yes, Captain. At first I didn't want to. I'm an old man with my own ideas. . . . I mean, it was unconstitutional. Then I figured that this was part of the 'new order' and I did it."

"That was a smart move, Mayor," said the officer. "You should be congratulated." His demeanor had now improved. "Was there any reaction from those of the opposition party?"

"No, no there wasn't, Captain," said the old man. "There couldn't have been. No one here is interested in these things. No one wants to work for the government. They say it's a waste of their time. They only care about their wives, their children, their sea, their boats, and their land, if they have it."

The officer was a bit surprised and, arching his eyebrows, he asked, "And our people?"

"Ours," said the old man, cracking his knuckles, "also live close to the land. They don't like this. Many of them don't come to work. They just come to collect their paychecks, and with some disdain, as if in doing so they are providing a great service for their country."

"They are strange people," said the officer as he crushed his cigarette in the ashtray.

"This town," said the mayor, "is very different from the Andean towns. Inland they have highways, there are cities that provide all kinds of services, and people are well informed. Here, the telegraph rarely works, the telephone hardly ever, and the only accessible route is the sea."

It was hot. The officer stood up and went over to the window. The window had glass shutters and looked out onto the street. He opened it. The yelling of some children entered freely into the room.

"They're playing," said the mayor. "There's no school."

The captain turned his back to the street without withdrawing from the window.

"There's a nice breeze here," he explained.

"The children," insisted the old man, "are happy. There's no school."

"I know," said the officer. "The troops needed the building."

"It's not because of the troops. School hasn't been in session for months . . . since the 'new order.' The teachers didn't belong to our party and there wasn't anyone else qualified to replace them."

The officer was not interested in the school situation, but continued the dialogue to keep the conversation going. He asked, "Does the commander know about this, Mayor?"

"Yes, I promptly informed him," said the old man. "I discussed it with the priest beforehand."

"With the priest, eh?"

"Yes, with the priest," said the old man. "I have to consult the priest on all matters of local government and administration according to the provisions of the 'new order.'"

The officer nodded without reply. The old man continued, "The priest agreed. He had never liked the woman teacher and he had had a disagreement with the male teacher regarding some books he was using, you know?"

"Yes," said the officer. "At the moment, schools are unnecessary. They are not so important. There are other more important issues."

"Schools," said the old man, "are important. Schools are not unnecessary, Captain. I have children; I know."

The officer approached. His eyes now shone with a strange glow and seemed to have grown larger.

"Let's not talk about schools," he said abrasively. "They don't interest me. We must think like the militants of a great movement and establish the 'new order,' supplanting, converting, or annihilating its enemies. The rest will come with time."

The old man, leaning back in his chair, watched him with bright, restless eyes. The officer continued his explanation.

"We will have to make sacrifices, but in the future we will reap the rewards. The party needs unconditional commitment from its men. . . ."

"Excuse me, Captain," interrupted the old man. "Would you like a glass of lemonade?"

"No, thank you. How's the water? Is it potable?"

"Not really."

"Is there a doctor?"

"No," said the old man. Then he added, stammering, "He had to leave . . . it was because of that incident with the pastor. . . ."

The officer knitted his brow as he wiped his neck with a handkerchief. The old man took out a folder. He said, "It's all here. Take a look."

The officer took the papers and looked through them rapidly. The title was "The Case of the American Missionary William Fischer." Then he placed them on the desk.

"I'll read them another time," he said.

The old man picked them up and started to look through them casually. Each page was a reminder of another difficult and unpleasant task. It began with a letter from the priest and ended with the disappearance of Mr. Fischer.

"The order from my superiors was unequivocal," the old man said, putting away the papers, "but it was against the law. I couldn't just send him packing, not without legal cause. It would have been disastrous. He was a foreigner and there are a lot of islanders in this town who share his language and religion. I considered making it a sanitation issue, but the doctor refused to certify it. On the contrary, he said that Mr. Fischer's school and chapel were the only clean places in town. So the priest, Gabino, and I organized a rally in which the fourteen men of the party and a few women took part.

"And the result?"

"Fantastic!" said the old man, lifting his hands. Then he added, "Of course it was. It was legal. It was 'the voice of the people.'"

The officer went back to the window and, from there, looking over his shoulder, he asked, "What's the priest like?"

The mayor peered over his glasses. Finally he stammered, "He's a fat old man. . . ."

"That's not what I meant," said the officer, waving his hand. "I'm referring to his stance, his ideas. . . ."

"Oh! Yes. He's good. He's with us. . . ."

"All of them are with us," said the captain. "It's our slogan. To impose and maintain the 'new order,' our party has on its side the two most powerful entities in the country, the military and the clergy. In other words, we are involved in a direct engagement preserved and protected by spiritual leaders. We can't go wrong. . . ."

There was a pause. The old man brooded with his chin resting on his hand while the captain observed the activity out on the street. Suddenly, the captain turned around and said angrily, "You missed your chance."

"Chance? What chance?"

The officer persisted, watching him intensely and severely.

"The chance to have done something," he said, agitated.

The old man was bewildered.

"You don't understand? We are imposing our doctrine by means of repression, and, let's say . . . a little bit of violence, and you have missed your chance. . . . I'm referring to the Pastor Fischer case."

The old man looked down and started to write something on a piece of paper. Instead he said, "It was a delicate situation. I was ordered to act with caution. Remember, Captain, he was an American citizen."

"So what!" he exclaimed. "That wouldn't have made any difference, as in fact, it didn't. And in any case, that's what our diplomats are for. . . . Do you really think it's so difficult for us to outwit those big, overfed kids with a piece of gum or chocolate always in their mouths? If you had gone through with it," he continued after a brief pause, "this town would now be ours."

"This town, Captain," said the old man softly, "is ours. Don't we rule over these people?"

"Rule, yes. But we need them in the party. There must be only one party, without opposition. If you had gone through with it, we would have already gotten rid of the most stubborn ones, and the rest would have changed sides and joined our ranks. Understand?"

"I'm an honest man," said the old man. He had let his guard down, despite himself.

The officer looked at him with surprise and compassion. Then he made a rapid, disapproving gesture and sat down, crossing his legs.

"I have something for you," he said, taking an envelope out of his military bag. "Read it."

The old man unfolded the paper and his eyes scanned it from top to bottom. His gaunt hands shook at first but then recovered.

"I've been removed from office," he said as he threw the envelope onto the desk.

"I'm sorry," said the officer.

"Don't be sorry, Captain," said the old man, smiling opaquely. "This is of no consequence, and it's doing me a favor. As I understand it, you will be replacing me. Right?"

"Yes. That is the order. I will be the civil and military commander of the town."

"So," said the old man, "the mayor's office is yours. I can sign over power whenever you like, Captain."

"We'll do it in the morning. You, of course, will be given another mission."

"A mission?"

"A mission within the party. The party directorate needs to be reorganized. You will be in charge of that."

The old man thought for a moment. Then he said, "May I decline?"

"Yes," said the captain calmly. "You may decline. We can all choose to decline. However, the party knows how to reward the worthy and punish the lazy."

"Listen, Captain," said the old man. "There are no politics in this town. There never have been. People say, 'I'm this,' 'I'm that.' They just say it, without repercussions, without conviction, without the necessary drive to defend their position. Instead of a political committee, why not create an aid commission to found a hospital or a school?"

The officer did not answer. He bowed his head. He knew what he had to say, but he didn't want to say it. Then he lifted his head and saw the old man's eyes—sweet, ancient, questioning—observing him closely.

"You are a stubborn man," the officer said and smiled. It was his first smile and his demeanor had also become strange.

"All of us old men," he replied, "are stubborn. At least that's what they say. But listen: we old men can give some good advice. Now that I'm not mayor anymore, I can offer you this service, freely and as a friend."

"Thank you," said the officer, nodding his head sympathetically.

"We have prepared a bedroom in my house for you, Captain. I'd like you to have it. You'll eat and live well at my home. My wife and I will treat you as if you were our son."

"You are very kind," said the officer. "But I cannot accept. It's part of my mission. I must live with my troops."

"It's up to you," said the old man. He straightened up some papers and stood up.

The officer began to get up slowly, and then he suddenly became very rigid. His gleaming and fanatical eyes had locked onto that face, onto the harsh features of the man whose portrait hung on the wall, behind the mayor's chair.

"That is 'the man'!" he said excitedly. "For him we must fight, conquer, or die!"

The officer remained rigid, with his legs stiff and his buttocks squeezed tight. His feminine countenance had transformed. The old man looked at him and thought, *He's crazy.* Then he looked at the portrait, at the man with the hard face, and noticed, unsurprised, that he was still smiling.

"See you around, Captain," he said, and he left.

Family Birthday Wishes

Germán Espinosa

"Hello?"

"Leonardo? It's Berta. I've been trying to call you all morning."

"I went grocery shopping. How are you?"

"Did you think I had forgotten?"

"About what?"

"About your birthday, silly. I sent you a little gift yesterday."

"Oh, yeah. Those lovely little guns. It's exactly what I wanted. Thank you. I tried one out this morning."

"You're welcome. And, by the way, happy birthday."

"Thanks, sis. I'm hearing a lot of noise in the background. Where are you?"

"Not far from where you are. At Heroes' Circle. I'm in my car. It's a beautiful day."

"Where are you headed?"

"I'm going to do a job. By the way, did you hear that Papa was killed last night?"

"Oh, yeah. Before going to the grocery store, I stopped by the medical examiner's office to identify the body. They didn't leave much for the mortician."

"Do they have any idea who did it?"

"The police think it was the Atuestas; they couldn't pay him back the money he had lent them. But I'm not so sure."

"Me neither. I'm thinking it was Mama."

"Well, I suspected her too, but . . ."

"Look, Leonardo, I know you're thinking that she really loved him. Imagine. Thirty-five years of marriage."

"That's what I thought. . . ."

"It's true, she loved him very much. Remember that time someone tried to bump him off at the soccer stadium?"

"Vaguely, yeah."

"She thought he was going to die. And it almost seemed as if she couldn't live without him."

"Sure, sure. It probably wasn't Mama."

"But it was, Leonardo. It seems they made her an offer she couldn't refuse."

"How much, more or less?"

"About a hundred million. Even I wouldn't have turned that down."

"Right. But, in any case, the old man was getting on in years. And he had had a very good life."

"Sure. And with all that money, Mama will be able to go on a good spree at Titi's, like she's always wanted to."

"Ah, that passion of hers for gambling. How she gets carried away."

"But it's her only weakness. Why shouldn't she indulge?"

"Okay, you're right, Berta. Especially with the price the Asprillas have put on her head."

"Of course; she could be done in any moment now."

"They've been talking to me, by the way. But the offer was too low. After all, one's mother is one's mother."

"How much did they offer you?"

"Very little. And I had already been hired to kill a politician around that time."

"They came to me, too. And I think Papa as well."

"Papa mentioned something about it. But they were offering next to nothing."

"Yeah, almost nothing. I preferred to take on the Aguirre contract. Remember? The car bomb uptown."

"Oh, yeah, of course. And that reminds me, Berta. I've been hired for one next Monday."

"Uncle Jose died in the car bomb uptown. Tough luck."

"Yes, I was at the wake. He was in pieces."

"Uncle Jose had been working for the Aguirres as well. They told me you turned down a job for them."

"It's a matter of principle, Berta. They didn't want to use Ecuadorian dynamite. I have an arrangement with the suppliers in Ecuador."

"I did, too, at one time. But now they're bringing over this marvelous gelignite from Holland."

"I'll have to try it. By the way, did you know that it was Papa who planted the bomb at the foreign ministry? I think it was his last job."

"Second to last. After that, he kidnapped the attorney general."

"I had forgotten. He must have really enjoyed knocking him around, because the attorney general had never paid him for the car bomb at the railroad company."

"That car bomb was a big mistake. The railroad company was offering a lot more to kill the attorney general."

"What are you talking about, Berta? I killed him."

"Good money?"

"Fifty big ones. They paid for my vacation in Miami."

"That reminds me, my visa has expired, but I'm friends with the consul."

"Me too. I met him at a reception in Nariño Palace."

"But, of course! I remember seeing you there. That was the day I spoke with the president about the bill to protect the business."

"That was it. The consul said there wouldn't be any problem with me, but he told me about what a nuisance those intellectuals are, applying for their visas."

"A menace. They claim they've been invited by universities when what they really want is to stay there illegally."

"Are you planning a trip anywhere?"

"You bet, little brother. I'm going to Israel. They're thinking of making me the middleman for a shipment of arms to the guerrillas."

"I was contacted by some people in France. But it looks like the guerillas can't afford them."

"That might change. They've managed some really good kidnappings over the last few months."

"Perhaps. Listen, Berta, I'm getting a lot of static."

"Yeah, I'm getting out of the car. There must be a lot of interference around here."

"Is your job going to take long?"

"Not really. Why do you ask?"

"We could eat dinner together."

"I don't think so. I'm planning on going to the funeral parlor tonight, even if it's just for a moment."

"We could go together."

"I doubt it, Leonardo."

"But why not?"

"Because by that time, you'll probably be at the medical examiner's."

"Me? But I was just there this morning."

"Well, you'll be there for something different."

"What?"

"The attorney general's family has been very generous, little brother."

"What do you mean?"

"Look behind you, Leonardo."

He turned his head and saw her there, silhouetted in the doorway. Her left hand still held the cellular phone to her ear. In her right hand, she held the submachine gun. He didn't even have time to panic before the blast annihilated him.

Fear

Manuel Mejía Vallejo

"They should be here soon," the old man says, drying off his brown face with a dirty towel. "Hopefully they'll be less brutal."

His voice becomes a plea, lost now in the damp folds of the towel.

Outside his café, boots march to the beat of Sergeant Mataya's piercing voice: "Haaaalt!" he shouts, and the pavement is burned by the fierce stomping of heels. The soldiers' faces shine with sticky perspiration under the midday heat. Browned with dust and fatigue, they stiffen their muscles at the sergeant's command.

The old man is no longer shaving. The steel blade of the razor trembles in his hand.

"My beard needs a rest anyway."

He removes the soapsuds from his face with the towel, with which he also rubs his eyes.

The soldiers will again fill his establishment with voices. He also will be filled with voices. Everywhere terror mounts: in the blades of the bayonets, in the steady march of the troops, in the silence of every corner, in the impossible response. Before, the sounds were those typical of a village with doves in its streets. Now, he hears military vehicles, the sharp orders of the commander, gunshots. The doves display their love uneasily on the rooftops; they seldom fly to the deserted streets.

He wraps the towel around his neck and with weariness in his voice he says to his wife, "What are we going to do? We have to make a decision. Our son already did."

She sustains a desperate silence.

They look nervously at the same spot. One day the bomb appeared. "Who could have brought it here?" the old man asked himself. They could kill a whole squadron of soldiers with it. "It was my son. He sent it because the revolution is expanding. He hoped that I, too, would make up my mind."

That was two months ago. The old man didn't agree with his son. He didn't turn him in, nor did he allow the bomb to be used; he kept it for no particular reason in a box of potatoes.

Now it's constantly bursting under its stringent obligation to explode in front of Sergeant Mataya and his soldiers. Thinking of the possible assault, his old leathery face goes pale, his movements get clumsy. What is he waiting for? The presence of the soldiers terrifies him. "At least before, we lived, we listened to the radio, read the newspaper, got together with old friends to talk about days gone by. Or we were silent, without much concern."

Again he hears the heels striking pavement, the shouted orders, and the rhythmic march in the middle of the street, until the squadron has become something amorphous in the ears of the old man. The towel has been lowered from his face to his neck inside his unbuttoned shirt.

"Are they the new soldiers?" asks the woman. Her husband begins to clean the bar with an old rag.

"The new ones arrive tomorrow. I don't know how we've stood it."

"Maybe they won't be worse, Jacinto."

The soldiers are not bad people. They have orders. But orders and soldiers have become one and the same thing for the townspeople. Soldiers are things that carry pistols and rifles and bayonets, that bloody their boots with the gaping flesh of guerrillas.

The sound of boot heels shifts from the cobblestones of the street to the brick of the sidewalk to the wooden planks of the establishment. Heavy soldier boots. Acrid, oozing fumes, thick green drill jackets, sharp gray weapons, furrowed eyes, brusque gestures. Whirlwinds breathing like animals.

The old man twists the towel in his hands.

The interior darkens as the uniforms appear panting against the door. Shadows gyrate on the splintered floor.

"We're tired. The usual," says Sergeant Mataya. He wants to order *aguardiente* and say that they couldn't track down the guerillas.

Sergeant Mataya, a name worthy of his stature. Wide mouth of powerful teeth. Hairless jaw aggressively set. Resolute eyes, devoid of brows. Prominent cheekbones to tighten his skin of old copper.

"They will all fall!" he rasps. "That son of yours is a damn fool."

"He's just a kid, . . ."

Sergeant Mataya stares at him. The old man repeats "just a kid . . ." as if in solidarity. Terror begins to override his survival instinct. The moment has come when he is indifferent to everything.

He could destroy them with the bomb he keeps in the box of potatoes. A little God. He has to decide on his destiny, on that of his present circumstances, on that of those who would be affected by his act. He is overwhelmed at having so many options, which used to always be in the hands of others.

"Are you nervous, Jacinto?"

He detests Sergeant Mataya's questions more and more.

"Why are you sweating so much, old man?"

"It's hot."

The sergeant chafes him with his eyes, takes a look around, and wipes his whole head with a large gray handkerchief.

"It's hot."

The idea floats in the air: under this kind of climate it seems that everything must end in death, that one lives a death of sweat stuck to one's skin like heat to a flame.

The sergeant gets up, sucking in his vast chest as he exclaims, "This damn town! Morning, day, and night. It's hot all the time. If there were only a little wind!"

"Towns become unbearable. Maybe that's why people are going up into the mountains. . . ."

"Damned guerillas. We'll get them all!"

The tip of his cutlass surreptitiously grazes the ribs of a soldier. A furtive look gives away the old man's nervousness.

"Don't take your eyes off him. He's up to something."

Conspiracy has inundated the air. The rag is wrung anxiously in the old man's hands. His eyes flit from the shelves to the soldiers, from the soldiers to the box of potatoes, from the box to the door, from the door to the box.

"Do the gentlemen want something to drink?"

Today his son is fighting in the mountains with his solitude on his sleeve. His son is a guerrilla, an outlaw; they want his remains under their boots, as if by killing a man, you can kill off the fear.

"Come here, old man."

He looks at the box of potatoes out of the corner of his eye as he obeys Sergeant Mataya's request. In his spasmodic smile pulsates the fear of decision. He must discover his universe for himself, confront its anguish, feel its torments. No one can help him because in facing his own fears, he will always be utterly alone.

A soldier gets up and the old man sits in his chair. With cat-like movements the soldier heads for the stack of potatoes; he looks over the scattered merchandise, the shelves of dry goods and bottles of cheap liquor. Sergeant Mataya and the old man watch the slow movements of the soldier as he completes his inspection. The old man squeezes the rag in his hands.

"These damn people are up to something!" roars Sergeant Mataya, peering out the door. "What the hell are you scheming, old man?"

Silence in the smoldering air. Silence on the roofs without doves. Silence in the closed doors. And in the deserted streets, and in the guitars, and in the eyes of children.

Silence.

"All of you will pay for this, old man. You know more than you're saying."

"Sergeant," says the soldier with cheerful submission. "I found it in the box of potatoes."

"Aha! Where'd you get that bomb, Jacinto?"

He grabs the old man's shirt with his enormous fists and crushes him against the wall.

"If you don't talk, I'll kill you. What are those bastards up to?"

"They're good people, Sergeant. They're desperate. They have to live somehow."

"What for?"

With one shove he throws the old man against the bar, and then he heads for the door of his establishment. One of the soldiers stops him. The sergeant says with precarious calm, "Bring over a full bottle. We have to talk, Jacinto."

The owner's eyes tremble, and he obeys.

"What do you know about your son?"

"My son made up his mind. I never agreed with him, but a man's got to make up his mind when the time comes."

Make a decision. That was the problem. The eternal problem that every man must confront. He, and he alone, must face it. No one will make it for him; no one can rid him of his anxieties because one can't rely on others' experience in matters of conscience. History is useless when it comes to one's own destiny. He has to choose a life, and within those parameters, act, decide.

The sergeant takes out a stack of dirty papers.

"Look at these newspaper clippings. Criminals, all of them."

"Yes," concedes the old man, "the moral compass has been smashed. There's nothing left but vengeance on either side."

Today his son is fighting in the mountains; at least he has a path to clear. He, on the other hand, sees all of his routes closed off. This conviction makes him so angry it scares away his diffidence. "Do you have any idea what a town is capable of when it is overcome with fear?"

The tone of his voice sounds strange in the group. Sergeant Mataya studies him.

"What's wrong with you, old man? Have a drink with us. It could be your last."

"With you guys anything could be the last."

"Did the smell of *aguardiente* go to your head, old man?"

They laugh raucously. The old man smiles, the corners of his mouth quivering.

"Tell me, haven't you ever felt fear, I mean real fear. I have. When

I see you, when I hear you coming, when you come inside, when you leave . . ."

Sergeant Mataya slams his hand on the table. The bottle starts to fall and the old man hurries to grab it, watching wide-eyed as the liquid slides down the floorboards. His trembling hand fills the glasses, more transparent now with the liquor.

"Cheers, old man!"

"Cheers, Sergeant Mataya."

"Cheers!" everyone says, and they raise their arms, and after their arms, their glasses, and after their glasses, the wedges of lemon, and after the lemon, the acrid looks on their burning faces.

"It burns the gullet."

"It burns."

The clicking of tongues savors the tension.

"Have you heard anything about my son?"

The old man pronounces the boy's name with pride. For the first time he doesn't feel fear at naming him. A raw tenderness comes over him from the words that remind him of that premature fullness of his son's beard, at the foot of the mountain.

"We'll get him sooner or later. All of those bandits will fall!" shrieks the sergeant. "And when I get my hands on them . . . !" He furiously squeezes the neck of the bottle as if to strangle it.

"Like this, like this! Until not a drop of life is left."

He tips the bottle over all of the glasses.

Sergeant Mataya. Dangerous man when fighting for a cause that is deemed worthy of crime, that authorizes bloodshed without affecting the conscience. The fanatic, the follower of orders in which criminal acts are seen as the only solution, sanctioned not to allow one's conscience to interfere with the final analysis. And the orders are unconditional: get rid of the guerrillas. He is delighted that the fulfillment of his duty is so intimately connected with iniquity. It is no longer a question of cold deference to military orders but rather of passion in destruction.

"Why is the door locked, old man?" yells one of them.

"In case the bandits come. . . ."

He is mocking them. There is now a moral force behind his movements, in the old look in his eyes. They vaguely sense this. Sometimes it's easier to be courageous than to be afraid. Sometimes, fear is simply an expedient for courage, a containing wall for animal audacity. To be able to make the decision when the time comes.

"I was against all that: Against the guerrillas. Against violence. Against my son."

He again pronounces his name as a kind of rectification.

"They told me a lot of things. I didn't believe them. Remember, Sergeant Mataya? One day one of your soldiers shot a dove. That's when we knew that death had arrived in this town."

He looks at the soldiers a bit hazily and smiles with pain in his words: "My son went to the mountains to fight against you. One day you will kill him. I will be proud of his cadaver. . . ."

"The old man got drunk!" says one of the soldiers with a slight contortion of his belly.

"Haven't you ever said to yourselves, 'I'll be dead soon'? You die a little at a time when you're afraid, until you say to yourself, 'Now I'm going to die completely.' And then you're not afraid anymore, and you're almost happy."

"We've faced death so often, we've gotten used to it."

"Because we men have much of the gambler in us and we think that everyone else will die, except 'me.' We drive away fear in a game of chance in which luck is on our side. But, what if we had the absolute certainty that we were going to die, like now?"

"We're soldiers. We're prepared to die."

"Man will never be prepared to die, because he never wants to, because . . ."

He doesn't finish. He stares at Sergeant Mataya. His son could be there in his place. Peasant stock, following orders. Everyone has their problems. Children, mothers, basic necessities. He feels like crying.

"Cheers, Sergeant Mataya."

With the glass next to his lips, his eyes cloud over. But the cruelty of a cornered man prevails and he repeats, "I was against my son."

"That's why you're here to tell about it, old man."

"I thought that the government wanted peace. I collaborated with you. But I understood what terror was when I saw you act. Everything has gone bad for us under your boots. Everything has changed for the worse under your guns and your disdainful voices. Men avert their eyes, women don't go out, children cling to their mothers' skirts or those of their older sisters. Before there was hope; we liked to listen to the girls laugh. Now with you everything has been lost."

The soldiers look at him with wild and furious eyes. They're waiting on Sergeant Mataya, a man who always knows what to do. The old man, once so fearful, has now become fearless. A brief, surprised silence is filled with the sound of gunshots outside of town.

"Do you hear the gunshots, Sergeant Mataya? It's my son, who's coming with his men. He made up his mind when the time came. It's a man's duty to decide when the time comes. . . ."

They prick up their ears and brace themselves for the encounter at the outskirts of the town.

"Old fool! You've kept us here talking while I should have been out there on the offensive. You'll pay for this soon enough, you and your son. All of the guerrillas will fall and not even their skin will be left on them. This is how I'll squeeze them," he says as his powerful fists wring the hat on one of the soldiers, who has bent his head. "Let's go!" he adds with authority, securing his belt riddled with cartridges. They move reluctantly, as if this were their last escape.

Pointing, with grief in his eyes, the old man says, "You will be the first. Then him, and him, and me. And you, Sergeant Mataya. Don't you think it's a little too late? Your plan has failed. In a minute we will all be dead."

Hands, glasses, eyes freeze.

"Do you understand now what it is to be afraid? I poisoned the liquor; there's no escape, I can assure you. Here, and in the other cafés of the town as well. We have been pushed into a corner with no way out. You see? My hand is shaking. I see very poorly now. Everything is so sad. . . ."

They don't hear his last words. Only the old man remains seated, bitterly serene. The others writhe, looking for the door, a shelf, water. They start to scream; they take out their guns and throw them savagely. There is no hatred for the old man, only terror before death and no way to fight it. It bores through them, taking them over. It is filling them up, like a glass that ceases to be a glass when it overflows: they are death, in contortions and screams of useless struggle, without time for resignation, without a pause to reflect. An animal survival instinct is there, but sunk into a bottomless abyss that plucks the eyes out of their sockets and contracts their hands and turns their fingers into claws to cling to a shred of life that flees from them in their desperation.

"Listen to the gunshots in the streets, Sergeant Mataya. It's my boy who's coming into the town that you have ruined. Do you know how many guerrillas there are?"

Sergeant Mataya wrestles with the bar on the door, one of his hands pressing against his stomach, contorting now under the pain of the poison in his bowels and coursing through his veins.

The door opens when Sergeant Mataya falls against it in raging pain. The footsteps of the guerrillas are nearing the door. Sergeant Mataya's gun falls from his hand, inert on the cobblestoned street.

The old man wants to see his son, but his eyes refuse to respond. He knows that his son will step over the sergeant's body, which lies stretched across the doorway out onto the pavement outside.

"I made my decision, son," says the old man haltingly, his sight already clouded. "My hand is shaking a little . . . ," he concludes, resigned to death, to everyone and everything dying with him, with his agony.

The Designator

Roberto Montes Mathieu

I crept up behind him and firmly touched his shoulder. Pallid, he slowly turned around only to find my smiling face. "Oh, it's you!" he said, and he tried to laugh but only managed to produce a ridiculous grimace. I took him by the arm and we walked under the harshness of the mid-afternoon sun. I was going to say, "It's hot, isn't it?" But when I saw he was dressed in tweed, indifferent to the climate, I stopped myself. "How's it going?" he asked, and with a movement of my hand I told him so-so.

We went into a café and ordered coffee and water. Watching him bring the cup to his lips, a strange feeling came over me that seemed to be compassion. And if what they said about him wasn't true? Maybe they had exaggerated; he didn't look like such a bad person. But still, appearances can be deceiving.

Seeing him up close, with his well-groomed black mustache in contrast with the two-day-old stubble on his face, and the somewhat listless look in his eyes behind the dark sunglasses, he didn't stand out in the least. Except for his solitude, the constant urge to be alone.

He always greeted everyone at the office, out of pure deference and because of that Andean penchant for appearing to be respectful and polite, but none of us would call him a friend. He was obliged to speak to us because we worked together, and even then we only talked about the particular job we were doing. He never spoke of his private life, nor did he allow any intrusions into it on anyone else's part.

Soon after starting to work with us, someone who had known him at another time and in another place told us who he really was. It was then that, driven by a morbid curiosity, I decided to try to get closer to him. A difficult task, considering how elusive and guarded he was.

I imagined him swathed in a tight raincoat, with the collar turned up and a hat tilted to one side like a gangster out of a movie, entering a restaurant, observing all of the tables, and then leaving to tell the hit men that the man they were looking for was seated next to the window dressed in gray with a red tie, then walking away while behind him the muffled detonations of the revolvers did what they had to do. Only he knew how many innocent people he had condemned to absurd deaths, and now perhaps he was afraid to end up like those poor wretches. That's why he didn't have any friends, that's why his interactions with people were limited to a simple greeting and on rare occasions, like with me, a cup of coffee and a casual chat about the office. Anyone could be out there seeking some overdue revenge.

Although I tried on several occasions to break through his hard shell, I only managed to get out of him that he was about to retire, that he was of the age and had put in enough years to do so, that he planned on using his pension to move to Venezuela where he had been told one could live more comfortably. "You wouldn't have a woman over there, would you?" I said, trying to establish some intimacy, but as always he laughed halfheartedly out of obligation and changed the subject to something trivial.

My friends thought I was going too far and they were amazed that I could sit and chat with him, or walk with him out of the office until at some point he would stop to say good-bye and continue on by himself.

"What a strange guy," we remarked. "He's scared of his own shadow." "I bet he doesn't even sleep." And trying to understand his way of life, we put ourselves in his place and realized that death could be lying in wait for him anywhere, even in an encounter with a complete stranger.

When I would surprise him from behind and put my hand on his shoulder, he would go rigid and cold and turn as white as a sheet. I would experience an unspeakable satisfaction, which I did my best to hide so he wouldn't shut me out. I was just a matter-of-fact kind of guy, he would think, and whenever I managed to surprise him like that, we ended up having a cup of coffee together.

Sometimes we sat facing each other, consuming our order in silence like two strangers sharing the same table, looking around us awkwardly. Then we would go out into the street, and at some point he would say his good-byes and walk on alone, like he is now, crossing the street in front of me to avoid getting splashed by a passing car, demonstrating how much he trusts me by turning his back, and I try to imagine the look of terror in his eyes when he sees me reaching for my gun.

Gelatin

Harold Kremer

Today I go to the office at six in the evening. The secretary says that Carepasa wants to see me. I go up to his office. He tells me to sit down. My feet hurt. I have blisters on one of them. Without looking at me he asks for the invoices, without looking at me he looks at them one by one and he takes notes in an account book.

"Only five boxes?"

"Only five," I answer.

He scratches his head. He picks up his pen and then he leans back.

"I think I'll send you to that training course. What did you do today, son?"

I spend the whole afternoon calling home from a pay phone. It's busy. I'm in the Santa Elena marketplace. I put down the phone and go to one of the stands. I present the product, give him the pitch: gelatin with a double dose of vitamin C. "It doesn't sell," answers an almost blind old lady. "We're at your service." I leave my card. I go back to the phone. Busy. I go to another stand. I shake hands with a greasy old man. "I still have the entire previous order," he points to the shelf. And there are the faded boxes. I go back to the phone and dial slowly. An eternity goes by. Busy. I want to go home and kill Ana.

"I covered the entire Santa Elena marketplace," I say. "About fifteen stands."

Carepasa doesn't take his eyes off of me. I stare back.

"Where do you think, son, the money to pay the employees comes from?"

I've never thought about it. It doesn't interest me.

"From the sale of bakery goods," I answer.

"Correct. . . . When a company as important as ours launches a new product into the market, it has to make an investment. Generally, you don't expect to make any money off of it for the first year. But, do you know how long we've had the gelatin out on the market?"

He makes a note in his account book.

"Tell me, son. . . ."

I hate the old bastard.

"Three years," I say.

"You are mistaken. They've been on the market for five years and we are the second largest manufacturer of gelatin in Colombia. Bogotá has the highest sales figures, Barranquilla is second, Medellín is third. . . . Do you know what place Cali is in?"

He makes another note in his account book. He's always making notes, keeping statistics, making charts. And he always asks me questions that I can't answer.

"Tell me, son. . . ."

"Fourth place. We're in fourth place."

"You are mistaken. We're in seventh place." He taps his head several times with his index finger. "Think for a moment: Do you think it's fair that the third most important city in the country is in seventh place?"

I say no with my head. But the old man wants to hear my voice and waits for an answer.

"Well, no. . . ."

I'm tired and I shift positions in the chair. I think of Ana. I want to get home and hear her say that nothing has happened.

"That's right, son. I have to send a report to Bogotá every month. And every month I am ashamed of our sales rate. Three years ago we were in second place. We struggled for every bakery, every shop; we convinced people that they needed our products . . . but first the salesman himself has to believe in the product. Tell me the truth: Do you consume Gelqueen in your home?"

He places his hands on the desk and observes me.

"We love it," I say. "Especially my little girl. She loves the tutti-frutti flavor. Sometimes I buy it right here."

My daughter hates Gelqueen. "It looks like rubber and tastes like paint," she says.

"That's good, son. A good salesman starts at home. I dream of the day when people can't live without Gelqueen. When that day comes we will be big. Understand?"

I move my head affirmatively and I again change position in the chair.

Then he gets up and goes to the small built-in bookshelf in the wall. He looks through a pile of papers and dusty books. He takes out a book and slaps it against the desk to remove the dust. The dust makes him cough.

"*The Best Salesman in America* by Doctor Pedro Mejía Arana."

On the cover is a map of North America and a smiling man, with glasses, holding a trophy.

"This book is our bible, son. You have to read it four or five times a year. I still read it."

I open it. It's a shitty little book with chapters like "What Is a Product?" "What Is a Customer?" "What Does It Mean to Sell?"

"Our bible," he repeats.

He sits down and observes me. I continue to page through it; I read the titles out loud. Carepasa smiles.

"You'll have time enough to read it; it's a gift. I want to make you into a good man, a great salesman. Now tell me: You're married, right?"

"Yes, Don Ismael."

"How many children do you have?"

"Just the little girl, Don Ismael. . . ."

"And your wife . . . ?"

My wife is the biggest whore in the Americas. Two weeks ago I discovered that she's having an affair with some shyster lawyer. She doesn't deny it but says that nothing has happened yet. According to Ana he is an interesting man with whom she talks about interesting things. And if nothing has happened yet it's because she loves me. Meanwhile, I go around wearing out pairs of shoes; my feet are becoming deformed, my blisters torture me, my head is a piece of gelatin. Last night she got home at one in the morning. She denied she had been with the lawyer. She left the university with some classmates and went to the Casona Bar for a few beers. She was drunk, but I didn't have the strength to keep her from sleeping, to start a fight, to wake up the kid.

"Her name is Ana," I say. "She's in law school . . . she's wonderful, a perfect wife . . . she loves our little girl and me. . . . I think that together we're really going to get somewhere in life."

"That's what I like to hear," says the bastard. "Later on, son, when you become a star salesman, the company will give you loans so you can buy yourself a house and a car. That's how I got my start thirty-five years ago. At that time I was a young man just like you . . . skeptical and rebellious . . . and now I am convinced that the family gives us happiness, the company well-being, and the State liberty."

Reminding me of Ana makes me bitter. I want to get up and strangle him, throw him out the window, cut his throat with a knife. He's been giving me this speech for three months now. When my wife stays out late and I can't sleep, I make myself think of nice things to avoid the bitterness. But few nice things have happened in my life. Then I hear Carepasa's voice and I can't avoid the bitterness anymore. Everything I hate begins to swarm around my head: gelatin, family, the company, the State. Then come my mother, my wife, and then once again, gelatin.

"Now go, son," he says. "Your family is waiting for you."

I go out into the street and go up San Nicolás to Fifteenth Avenue. Overflowing buses. Cars. Vendors. Thieves. Prostitutes. I clutch my knife and cross the avenue. My feet hurt.

Today I arrive at the office early. Carepasa wants to see me. I give the invoices and the briefcase to the secretary and I tell her that I'll be right back. I go to the university. It's Friday and I need to speak with Ana. I ask the guard where the law school is. He looks me up and down.

"Which year?"

"First year."

"Which classroom?"

I don't know. He tells me that there are seven first-year classrooms. I try to go in and he stops me. He's a puny Indian with a sly face.

"I need to speak with my wife. My mother-in-law is in the hospital and she could die at any moment."

He claims that I need a student ID card. It's an order from the rector's office. There are rumors that the guerrillas want to take over the university.

"What about my mother-in-law?"

He speaks with another guard. He asks for my national ID card and he frisks me. He finds the knife, a switchblade that I always carry.

"To defend myself against thieves," I explain.

The other guard also frisks me.

"So?"

"Go ahead, but I'll keep the knife here for you."

I go to the classrooms and look inside from the doors. Sixty, seventy students per room: everyone is talking about family, laws, and society. I walk through the corridors; I read the notice boards. I want to barge in on her and the lawyer. Finally I go back for my knife and go to the café across the street. There's nowhere to sit. They bring me a little stool. I don't recognize anyone. Everyone is yelling; everyone's getting ready to party, and the stereo muffles the voices. I order a beer. They start to leave at nine thirty. I pay and stand by the door. I wait for half an hour. Ana is not at the university. So I touch my knife and go down to the Casona Bar.

The bouncer doesn't want to let me in. He claims that there are no free tables, but I push him aside and go in. It's dark inside. I go from table to table; I go up to the couples dancing. Suddenly someone grabs my arm: it's the bouncer. I break free and clutch my knife.

"I told you there aren't any tables!"

"I know, asshole!"

He leaves and comes back with two waiters.

"We would like you to please leave, sir," says one of them.

I take out the knife and release the blade.

"Who's going to make me?"

Two women coming out of the bathroom see us and begin to scream. Instantly all of the women are screaming. The tables are emptied. I move forward, bracing myself with my feet wide. The waiters retreat. The music is turned off. I make a threatening gesture with the knife and they jump back. One of them takes a step forward and I strike him with the knife, almost slashing open his belly. The man recoils and falls on his back. Someone is saying something next to me.

"What's going on? What's going on here? What does he want?"

He approaches with his hands in front of his chest. I turn slightly. They're cornering me. He talks to the waiters.

"I'll speak to him . . . come on, man: what do you want?"

I vacillate between the group of waiters and the man. I see the lights reflected in the blade of the knife. I turn it over in my hand.

"This asshole insulted me!" I yell, pointing with the knife at the waiter.

The guy looks at them, signaling them with his head.

"We're very sorry, sir . . . anything you want is on the house, but I'm begging you to put away that knife."

I know the trick. Put away the knife, we'll all be friends, and then a medley of punches and kicks. I hear a siren. I step backward toward the door. There's a group of people gathered on the other side of the street. The siren is getting louder. I leave with the knife in my hand and everyone screams and runs. The police car isn't there yet. I run toward the university, three blocks up the hill. I jump over a fence and dive onto the ground. I wait for about an hour. The police car passes by several times. I wait for another hour. I walk alongside the university and I buy a bottle of *aguardiente*. I get home and, before opening the door, I know that the house is empty.

Today I get up at nine o'clock. I throw up and take four aspirin. The house is a disaster: dirty dishes, clothes strewn on the floor, trash everywhere. I open the freezer and there is no ice. Ana left me a week ago. She went to live with Angelita at my mother-in-law's house. I try to talk to her every day but she's never there. On Wednesday and Thursday I waited until late for her in the park across from my mother-in-law's house. The whore now lives in motels, with the lawyer. She left me a note saying that she wanted to be alone for a while. She talks about the future, our little girl, my alcoholism. I know that she didn't write it: the lawyer dictated it to her. I shower and dial the phone. It's her.

"I'm coming over there," I say. "I need to talk to you."

"I don't want to see you. A friend of mine told me what you did at the Casona. It's over."

"I want you to tell me in person."

"I don't want to see you!" she yells. "If you come, I'll call the police!"

I hear her breathing. She's frail.

"You're going to keep me from seeing my daughter!"

Silence. She tells me to wait. I hear voices in the background. I think that one of them is a man. She comes back to the phone.

"You can come."

Blood rushes to my head.

"That son-of-a-bitch lawyer is there!"

Silence.

"No . . . what's happening between us has nothing to do with him . . . he's only a friend."

"And since when do friends feel up their friends!"

She slams down the phone. I get dressed fast and run to flag down a taxi. Why aren't there any taxis in Cali on a Saturday at eleven in the morning? When my daughter sees me she runs to hug me. I love my little baby. She's five years old and I let her do anything she wants. My witch of a mother-in-law wants to pry her away from me. Angelita tells me about Ana: she sleeps late, she doesn't feed her, she's constantly on the phone. And if the kid demands something, like to play or to go out, she punishes her. I hate Ana. I'm always inventing games with Angelita. We go to the park. I ask her if Ana is at home. She presses her lips together and shakes her head. I see the curtain moving. I ask her again.

"It's grandma," she says.

And then she laughs. She lets go of my hand and runs to hide behind a tree. I lean against it and pretend that I'm crying for my lost daughter. Angelita appears with her arms open and we roll around the ground. We play that the park is a forest.

"Who am I?"

"You're a rooster lost in the forest," Angelita says, opening wide her eyes, showing her little teeth as she laughs.

And I make like a rooster. The witch is still behind the curtain. I jump and yell more fervently.

"What do roosters do?" I ask.

"They help the hens make chicks."

Angelita is very intelligent. She runs toward me with her open arms and we fall to the ground again. I sit her on my lap. An old man is watching us.

"Who's he?"

"An old man," she says. She brings her little face up to my ear; she cups it with both her hands and whispers, "He's watching us."

I get up and yell, "What the hell are you looking at, you old fag!"

The old man runs to the other side of the park. Angelita laughs. We sit down and she tells me the story of "The Little Mermaid." Then we lie down on the grass and find animals in the clouds. Suddenly the little girl whispers in my ear, "I saw Mama kissing a man."

My heart jumps. I close my eyes. I feel like I'm drowning. I begin to sweat.

"Who is it?" I ask with a suffocating voice.

"Mr. Gerardo . . . and . . . and Mama went away in a big car with him."

I go into the house and tell the kid to pack her things.

"The girl is not leaving!" shouts the witch.

She grabs her arm and pulls at her until she cries. I push the old woman. The kid screams. I take out the knife and put it up to her face.

"Let go of her or I'll cut you!"

She lets go of her. I take her to her room so she can pack. I go back to the living room. The old woman is crying. She wants to talk me out of it; she talks about clothes, food, education. She pays for Ana's clothes, Angelita's school, and sometimes the groceries. I yell that my daughter can't get a good education in a brothel, in a neighborhood full of fags.

The old woman runs to her room. I walk up and down the living room: imported porcelain; large, clean armchairs; rug under the table. I kick over a large vase. It shatters against the wall. I open the knife and plunge it into an armchair. I want to tear it but I can't. However hard I try, I only manage to make a small hole. Then I start to slash it with the knife. Then I continue with the others. I grab some soil from a flowerpot and I throw it onto the rug. I go to the kitchen and bring back a jug of water: I pour half of it onto the rug and I rub my shoes in it. I pour the rest of the water into the vents of the television. Angelita still hasn't come out of her room. I hear her screaming. The witch has locked her in her room.

"Papa, Papa!" she screams behind the door. "Grandma locked me in!"

She's with her. I tell her to let her out or I'll break down the door. She yells that the police are on their way. I push the door with my shoulder; I walk back two steps and I kick it in the middle. It shakes a little. I take a running start and smash against it with my shoulder, but I bounce off and fall to the floor. I get up and start kicking it again. I stop for a moment to catch my breath and then I see the policemen. One kneeling on one knee and the other standing, pointing their guns at me.

"Stop or I'll shoot," yells one of them.

Angelita is crying. I tell them that the girl is my daughter and that she's been kidnapped. They hesitate for a moment.

"Against the wall!" says the one who is kneeling. Angelita is still crying. The policeman insists, "Against the wall with your hands up!"

They frisk me and find the knife. The old woman opens the door and the kid runs into my arms. We go to the living room. I'm carrying my daughter. The witch screams when she sees the furniture. She says that I'm a degenerate, that I'm crazy. I scream that she's kidnapped my daughter. My mother-in-law wants them to take me in for damage to private property.

"This torn furniture and the broken vase, were they like this before?" I ask the kid.

We all look at Angelita. She says, pointing at my mother-in-law, "Grandma did it."

"She did it so she could blame me for it!" I add immediately.

A small group of people forms outside: I see the old fag and I wink at him. They put me in the back seat. They don't talk along the way.

Today I decide not to go to work. I call the office and tell the secretary, in a quavering and weak voice, that I'm dying of fever. She connects me to Carepasa. My voice shakes, for real, when I hear him. He wants to make a good man out of me. He gives me advice about the chills and the fever.

"Tell your wife to prepare you a hot toddy."

Since my health insurance card still hasn't arrived, he gives me the name of the company doctor. I pretend that I'm going to get a pen and paper, I cover the mouthpiece with my hand, and I listen. He's talking to someone.

"It's one of those salesmen . . . now he says he's sick. . . ."

He covers the mouthpiece and I can still hear.

". . . What do we have to lose if he only sells five boxes a week. . . ."

Then silence. I hear distant laughing. Then he tells me the address and tells me about the training course. He already enrolled me and it begins in a week. I use the trick of getting disconnected: as I'm speaking I hang up the phone. I get into bed. I haven't slept in three days. There are days when I can't even get to sleep drunk. I'm afraid. I hear the sounds of the night and I think that something terrible is going to happen to me, that the police are coming to get me or that some hit men are breaking in to kill me. My heart quickens. I pull the blanket up to my neck, close my eyes, and resign myself to whatever happens. When I manage to fall asleep I dream of scenes from my childhood, things that I can't remember afterward.

I go out at eleven o'clock and hire a cart. We load the refrigerator, the stove, the stereo, and the television. We go to a pawnshop. They give me two hundred thousand pesos. Then I go to Eleventh Street and ask for Chucho. They take me through tenement rooms, corridors, and holes in patio walls that lead to other tenements. It smells like crack, shit, and urine. I want a pistol with a silencer, but I don't have enough money. I negotiate for a revolver and twenty bullets.

Today is Wednesday. On Monday I went to Pacho's bar. A young whore sits down at my table. She looks good and I buy her a few beers. She's twenty or twenty-five years old and she's missing a tooth. I like her like that, missing a tooth, with her big, black eyes. She's short, well built, and when we're on our fourth beer she asks me if I want to go to bed with her. I tell her that I don't sleep with whores. She replies that she's not a whore, that she does it because she needs the money, and she tells me a story that includes husband, son, mother, brothers and sisters, rent money. It sounds like a soap opera. I smile. I order more beer and I repeat that I don't sleep with whores. We chat for a while and she leaves. She goes from bar to bar searching for a place to crash. After a while she comes back and sits down. We keep drinking.

"So?"

She looks at me with her big eyes and remains silent. I realize that she's high. I tell her that I'm a salesman and I vomit *The Best Salesman in America* on her. I explain what a commodity is and how to sell it. She listens carefully to me; at least I think she does. I convey to her that her problem lies in combining begging with prostitution.

"If you lived in North America you'd have someone to manage your business for you, someone to tell you what you should sell, how to do it, and how much to charge . . ."

María lights a cigarette.

". . . and that you can't go around begging, giving discounts."

She asks me how my salesman job is going. I think for a moment and I tell her the truth: badly.

"Gelqueen is pure crap. Whoever buys it for the first time never buys it again."

I explain to her that I'm looking into a job in a dairy company. I drink beer. My mood has lifted after the story I've just invented. I have often dreamed of an important post as a salesman. Perhaps my problems would be resolved; perhaps I'd be able to get back together with Ana and my little girl, I'd have time to go back to school, it would be . . . María is speaking to me.

"I'll charge you half price."

"I don't sleep with whores," I repeat. She continues to reduce the price. She's drunk, a little more than me. Finally she says for free.

"You pay for the room."

I pay the bill and take her home. When we arrive she falls asleep, with her clothes on. I undress her. She's not bad. She has a scar just above her belly button and another on her back. The scars look like zippers. I lie down next to her and I feel good, calm. I bring over a bottle of Ana's perfume and put some on her neck, her ears, and her shoulders. I hold her hand and I fall into a deep sleep. I wake up at dawn. María is still next to me. It's still dark outside. I go to the bathroom to urinate. Then I drink two glasses of water, go back to bed, and immediately fall asleep.

I wake up sweating at ten. María's gone. I look for her all over the house. I remember the revolver in the kitchen. It's still there. I put it in my briefcase and then quickly shower. I'm hungry; I'm in a hurry. I go up to Fifth Street. The bus is late and I'm about to call the whole thing off. But the bus appears.

The house is perfect. It's in front of a park and there are empty lots on either side. Neighborhood of the rich, property of the rich, streets of the rich, cars of the rich. I hate rich people. The guard goes to lunch at noon. I walk with my briefcase toward the mountains. I stop by a shop and drink a Coca-Cola and eat two cheese bread rolls. I try to think of other things: of my little girl, of Ana, of María, of Carepasa, of the bond the police inspector made me sign to get out of jail. I could see my little girl for three hours every fifteen days until family court decided otherwise. I couldn't go anywhere near my mother-in-law's house. "And the lawsuit for the kidnapping of my daughter?" I asked. "You have to file it in criminal court," he said. When they took me out of the cell, I saw Ana in the other room, for an instant, with the lawyer. If I didn't sign I would run the risk of being sued for making death threats and for damage to private property. I signed. They took me back to the cell. Soon they let me go.

I go to the park and don't see anyone. I walk to the house imagining Ana in bed with the lawyer, explaining to her her rights concerning our daughter. Then I'm filled with bitterness. I open the gate and ring the doorbell. The maid appears. I ask for Doña Francisca as I take out a manila folder from my briefcase.

"These papers were sent to Mr. Gerardo."

She wants me to pass them to her through the window. I tell her that the papers have to be signed; I have to take them back with me.

"Hurry up, I'm hungry!" I say. "I'm expected out in Aguablanca for lunch."

She hesitates for a moment. She opens the door. I push open the door with my shoulder and enter, removing the revolver from my briefcase. The maid falls back onto the floor. I hit her with the side of the revolver and I crush my finger in the process.

"Keep quiet or I'll kill you!"

I grab her by the hair but she twists out of my grip and takes off running. I pursue her to the maid's quarters near the kitchen. There she starts to scream, calling to Doña Francisca. When she sees me appear in her room, she gets up on the bed. She huddles in a corner, crying.

"Keep quiet or I'll kill you!" I repeat.

My voice cracks when I ask her how many people are in the house. Suddenly I'm out of strength and I sit next to her. I calm her down: I only want to steal.

"No screaming," I say, approaching her face. "How many are there?"

"Doña Francisca and me," she says. "The mister gets home at one." Could Doña Francisca have heard her screams? I place the revolver between her eyes. "She's sleeping," she says. That's very nice. It's noon and she's still sleeping. Fucking rich old lady. I get up and turn on the television at high volume. I toss her a blanket.

"You're going to stay here and watch the soap opera while I go upstairs. Put the blanket over you."

She pulls the blanket over her head. She begs me not to kill her, that the pesos, jewelry, and dollars are upstairs, that she won't report me. I grab a cushion and put it on her head. I push it down on her.

"Don't move."

I position the revolver and shoot. Her body stops moving.

From the door to the kitchen, I can see the maid's face. Blood drips down her neck. Her eyes are open, staring to one side. I go back and throw another blanket over her and sit down on the bed. There's a commercial on the television. I hear a ring and turn down the television. I'm sweating. It rings again. It's the telephone. Someone answers upstairs. I run to the living room and pick up the receiver. It's the lawyer. He won't make it home tonight; he has a lot of work to do. I know the work he does with Ana. I curse my bad luck. I sit for a few seconds and decide to go upstairs. The doors to the bedrooms are open. Doña Francisca is still on the phone. I go in when she hangs up. She's lying down, thinking about what a good man her husband is.

"This is a stick up!" I yell. "Keep quiet or I'll kill you!"

She rubs her eyes. She's well into her fifties, withered, stout.

"What do you want?" she says, swallowing hard. "There's money in my purse . . . and the jewelry is over there. . . ."

She points to a small chest.

"That's more like it," I say. "If you scream, I'll kill you. I only want the money."

I look through her purse. At least two hundred pesos. A bonus. I go to the jewelry chest: rings, bracelets, earrings. I ask her about the dollars.

"That's . . . all there is. . . ."

"Get up, you old hag!"

I grab her by the hair and I push the revolver into her ribs. I lead her to the wardrobe and make her open it.

"Those are only clothes," she says. "The jewelry and the money is all I have."

I push the barrel into her. I push it in hard several times. She's cornered against the wall.

"You want me to shoot you?"

She doesn't think I'm serious. I lift the revolver and hit her in the head with it. She doubles over a bit and lets out a squeal like a rat. I pull her up by her hair and I point the gun at her face. She points to a box. I throw aside the clothing and there, wrapped in plastic, is the wad, the dollars. Doña Francisca cries. I help her get up and lay her down on the bed.

"Don't worry," I murmur to her. "I'll be leaving soon."

I toss her the blanket.

"You just watch the soap opera while I leave."

I turn on the television at high volume. The news is on. They're reporting a massacre in Urabá. Seventeen dead. I sit on the edge of the bed and watch the news report. Doña Francisca is curled up into a ball, wrapped up in the blanket. I shoot her from behind. I turn down the volume a little and go to the bathroom to wash up.

Today I get up late. I call the office and tell the secretary that I'm still sick. She thinks that they're going to fire me. She wants me to talk to Carepasa. I hang up and get back into bed. María is asleep. Last night we drank at Pacho's until late. She wanted money; she wanted me to pay for the other night.

"I didn't even touch you," I said.

She doesn't believe me. She gets riled up and I tell her to leave. I call Pacho. He appears with a metal rod.

"I told you not to bother my customers."

She promises to behave, bows her head, and asks for forgiveness. She does the same with me. We drink a bottle and then we go home. María is drunk and yells in the street that she's a whore, that I can fuck her whenever I want. For free. When we get home I take her to the bathroom.

"You have to bathe," I say. "You smell like a whore."

She doesn't want to. I get under the shower with her and scrub her all over. I get Ana's perfume. She can hardly stand up. I corner her in the bathroom. I dry her thoroughly, put perfume on her, and make her put on some pajamas. We go to bed. I caress her and press against her body, squeezing her tight. And I immediately fall asleep.

María wakes up at noon. I'm about to leave. I tell her that I have to deliver an order. She's hungry. I go to the store for bread and soda.

"If you wait here I'll bring you food."

I buy the newspapers on the street. I go to Pacho's and ask for my briefcase. I take out the dollars, I put them into a bag, and I give them to him. I say, "These are hot, Pacho."

He looks into my eyes and winks.

"I don't know a thing," he says.

I go back to Chucho's. Rooms, corridors, holes. The smell makes me vomit. He's sitting on a leather armchair. In the semidarkness I can make out the silhouette of a woman. I only hear murmurs. Half an hour later they let me come in. Chucho makes a gesture and the two men who ushered me in disappear. The room is enormous, with high ceilings, full of boxes, televisions, stereos. Just below the ceiling is a small window through which a little bit of light enters. Chucho laughs. He's missing several teeth. He's short and skinny. He watches me for a few moments before speaking.

"What do you want?"

"I want something better . . . the nice one with the silencer. . . ."

I hand him the revolver and the jewelry. He turns around to look at them under the light from the little window. I assure him that they're worth more than five million pesos. Chucho laughs. He says that they're worth ten times less. I take them back, ask for the revolver, and say my good-byes. Chucho continues to laugh.

"Who's going to buy them from you?"

I tell him of a pawnbroker. He laughs again. There's a policeman looking for them at every pawnshop.

"I know," I say. "But at Joaquin's they take them through the back door."

He lights a cigarette, scratches his shoulder, and stares at me.

"Do you know who Francisca's maid was?"

"Who?"

"The maid . . ."

I'm speechless. Chucho takes a puff at his cigarette. I swallow hard.

"What are you talking about?"

Chucho smiles.

". . . people tell you things, you hear things, you ask around, and you guess the rest."

"So, who was the maid?"

"A policeman's sister," he says.

I look for a place to sit. There are no chairs. Chucho follows me with his eyes.

"Everything and nothing is known."

"Who else knows about this?" I ask.

Chucho laughs.

"No one knows," he says. "Not even me."

I want to go and I look for the way out. Chucho stops me.

"What do you want?"

I look at him. He's still there, sitting, with the cigarette between his fingers. He gestures for me to approach.

"The nice one with the silencer. . . ."

He gets it. He wipes it off with his shirttails. He removes the silencer and puts it back on.

"A real beauty."

He asks for the jewelry, the revolver, and three hundred big ones. He affirms that it's hot. I ask him to lower the price.

"Not a peso less and I've never seen you before."

I give him everything. The rest is with Pacho. He shows me how to cock it, to fire it, to remove the bullet from the chamber.

I go home. María is asleep. I wake her up and we eat. They called me twice from work. I lie down and turn on the radio.

Today I get to work early. I go up to Carepasa's office. He tells me to sit down, and asks for the doctor's note. I explain that I don't have it, that I didn't go to the doctor, that I didn't have any money to buy medicine. Carepasa scrutinizes me.

"That's serious, son. Why didn't you call me?"

I tell him about the messages I left with his secretary.

"I got them," he points out. "But I'm talking about the medicine."

I bow my head.

"I was too ashamed, Don Ismael."

He takes down a note and scratches his bald head.

"Go to work, son. Come to my office this afternoon. I have something for you."

I go up to Fifteenth Avenue and buy the tabloid *El Caleño*. There's the story. "Two Women Killed in a Robbery" is the headline. I read the whole thing. There is an investigation under way and there are suspects. They don't know anything, I think. I go to the Alameda marketplace. I give them the double vitamin C pitch, the exclusive tutti-frutti flavor, the box with an extra fifty grams. They don't even look at me. Maybe they know that Gelqueen is a piece of rubber, that it tastes like shit. Why do I persist? For Angelita and for Ana. If I make it as a salesman, I know that they will come back home. I promise myself to sell ten boxes, raise my average. I go to the Siloé marketplace and go from stand to stand. And I finally manage to sell a box of assorted flavors. A dwarf tells me that only rich people buy gelatin. I put the briefcase on his counter. I lean on one foot, then the other.

"It doesn't fill you up," he asserts.

I want to explain to him about the vitamins, the nutritional value, but I don't even try. Then he adds, "There are people up the hill there who don't even have refrigerators."

I look at the mountain: houses clustered together, unpaved roads. I order a beer and offer him one. The dwarf accepts a shot of *aguardiente*. He takes the bottle from under the counter and pours himself a double. I leave the briefcase there and go to a pay phone. Ana answers. I beg her not to hang up; I'm sorry and I'm calling to ask for her forgiveness.

"I want to see Angelita. . . . I miss her."

She says that she hates me, that I'm a degenerate, and that she's filed for a separation. I can see the kid in a week. I tell her that I love them, that I remember the good times. She answers that she remembers my drunkenness, the days without food, the unpaid rent.

"I'm getting better," I say. "I'm the sales manager now and I might be working for an insurance company . . . and what's more . . . I've put away some money for Angelita, for her clothes. I can bring it right over."

"If you come here, I'll call the police," she says.

Neither she nor Angelita need me. And if I go over there, she repeats, she'll call the police. She hates me and I disgust her.

"Alright," I say. "I know that I've behaved badly . . ."

Ana doesn't respond. I hear the television. It must be a new one.

". . . But I'm getting better. If you come back to me, I'll forgive you for the lawyer."

She insults me. She repeats that I disgust her. Then I'm furious and when I begin to yell, she hangs up the phone. I call back. Busy. I go back to the dwarf and order another beer. I invite him to another shot. My feet hurt. I hate being a salesman.

I spend the afternoon at Pacho's drinking beer. Every so often Pacho says something like "It's hot" or "Look after the bar while I go to the bathroom." I know that he was a tough guy once, that he had done time and then had opened up this bar. He has a heart murmur and doesn't drink or smoke.

"What are you thinking about so much?"

I smile. I'm getting drunk.

"Women," I say.

I spend the afternoon thinking about how I will do it. It has to look like an accident. I could cut loose the brakes on the car, but I don't know anything about cars. I ask Pacho.

"What do you want to do?"

I don't answer. He adds that it doesn't work to cut loose breaks here. Not in Cali, because it's flat. Maybe they would get in an accident, but that's all.

"Never do things half assed," he adds. "Always take the surest path."

I'm getting drunk and I order more beer. I think of Angelita when she was born, of Ana when we got married. I lay my head down on the table and I sleep.

I jump when someone shakes me: it's María. It's almost six o'clock. I wash my face. María wants to come with me. I grab her hair and shake her and she kicks me. Pacho comes up with the steel rod. When she turns to look at him, I slap her. I leave and flag down a taxi.

Carepasa comes down to open the door. He asks how my day went. I put the invoice on the desk.

"Only one box?"

He leans back in his chair and crosses his arms.

"Do you know how much it costs us to take a box of gelatin up to Siloé?"

I don't intend to answer. I don't know; it doesn't interest me. He calculates gasoline, time, driver's salary, car wear and tear: all of that costs more than the box.

"It's not my fault!" I say, raising my voice. "I was assigned the poorest neighborhoods in Cali!"

Carepasa makes a note. He looks at me and writes something down again.

"They don't even have refrigerators in those neighborhoods!"

"Calm down," he says. "You smell like alcohol. . . . Were you drinking during work hours?"

I don't answer. He puts down his pen. He opens the box to his right and takes out an envelope. Then he opens the box in front of him and takes out a few pieces of paper. He hands me the envelope. It's addressed to me. They no longer need my services, says the letter, due to the downsizing of the company. I toss it onto the desk.

"I'm sorry, son," he says. "I wanted you to stay but your sales rate hasn't helped. And . . ."

He stops for a moment. He turns back pages in his account book.

". . . We checked out your reports. Some of the stands don't even exist. Others never saw you before."

He approaches and hands me the document of dismissal.

"Sign this."

I sweep everything off the desk with my hand. Carepasa gets up, afraid. He picks up the phone. I go up to him with the gun in my hand and hit him over the head with it.

"No telephones, asshole!"

He's bleeding. I push him onto the floor and place my foot on his stomach. I aim the gun at him with both hands.

"You bastard, Carepasa!"

I press down my foot and bring the gun closer to his face.

"Say that Gelqueen is shit!"

He says it.

"Your wife is a whore!"

He cries. He begs me not to kill him. He swears that he understands me, that we can start over. He offers me a raise, and home and car loans. I sink my foot in more.

"You can take what you want! The money is downstairs. I swear I won't turn you in!"

I kick him.

"I'm not a thief, you moron!"

I hit him again. He crashes against a leg of the desk and goes still. Then he coughs. He looks at me. I fire three clean shots: one for the company, one for the family, and one for the State.

I sit in his chair and look through the account book: telephone calls, sales figures, calculations, drawings. I sweep off everything that's left on the desk. I put the gun down. The desk is made of wood, dilapidated. You have to push and pull to open the drawers. Paper and more paper. I throw everything onto the floor. I lay my head down on the desk. My breathing mists the glass. The gun is a few centimeters away. I pick it up and put it up to my head. I close my eyes and begin to squeeze the trigger. Before doing it I want to speak with Ana. I dial the number. Angelita answers.

"Hello . . . Hello . . ."

My voice gets caught in my throat. Someone is speaking in the background. I can't identify the voice. Ana gets on the phone.

"Hello . . . Hello . . . Who is it? Hello . . ."

I can hear the voices again. I cover the mouthpiece. Ana says, "It's not him, honey. He would have talked to Angelita."

I hang up. I get up and put the gun in my briefcase. I turn off the light. They are waiting for me.

The Procession of Shadows

Germán Santamaría

The sun had already set when, from amidst the uncertain darkness of the night, José Durango saw the stream of light. He thought that the sky of the long previous nights had opened up and that what twinkled in the distance were fallen stars.

He remained still, watchful, under the lifeless shadow of a Saman tree. The lights drew closer and with them the murmur of voices. They were not stars but torches and the murmur came from the devotions of the procession.

He waited stealthily, no longer breathing in the smell of battle but that of the incense of the procession of shadows. He lay on his side underneath the Saman tree and felt the procession drawing still closer because its murmur was now a shattering clamor, and he saw the candle and torch flames growing.

The first line of the procession came and went. He did not see priests or acolytes or saints or crosses. He thought that the procession had not been convoked, was not led by anyone. It was merely the procession of the nameless.

They passed by ceaselessly right there in front of him, but he was unable to identify any of their faces. They were pale faces, transparent like wax. But they were not grim or sad faces. They carried with them the radiant gravity of a strange triumph.

More and more walked by and he saw that there were thousands of them and his apprehension grew because he could not recognize any of the faces, he could not name anyone, point to a body with his

hand, feel the redemption of someone's eyes on him. But no one recognized him; nor did José Durango recognize anyone in that procession of shadows.

He remained there motionless, waiting for something. Then he
saw Olimpo Cruz. He immediately recognized him as his Aunt
Matilde's boyfriend. Still only a child at the time, José Durango
often used to go with his aunt to bring flowers to Olimpo's cross,
under a walnut tree. The police had beheaded him along with a hundred others on the same day, during The Violence.

And now, next to Olimpo, he watched the twenty-one of Head-
less Peak walk by. They were the first cadavers he had ever seen and
then he remembered how, at only nine years of age, he had climbed
up to the Peak on the following day and seen the corpses face down
at the bottom of the ravine of red earth. They were naked and their
clothing drifted in the wind, hanging from the dry branches of the
nearby Guamo trees. And there they were walking in silence, with
candles in their hands, the twenty-one of them, the decapitated of a
long-ago morning.

He followed them with his eyes until they disappeared in the distance, amidst the throngs that continued to pass by, amidst the
crackling of the torches and the fumes of hot wax and the sperm
color of the faces of the marchers. Until he began to recognize the
faces of the bombing of Las Rocas. He instantly remembered that he
had seen everything, as an adolescent, from the Tierradentro Mountains. There, on the other side, between the gigantic rocky gorges
over the crag of the Recio River canyon, the government planes
sketched curves in the air and you could hear the thunder of the
bombs, and clouds of smoke rose in the wake of the burning coffee
plantations and ranches. The bombing lasted for several days, and
afterward the survivors brought stretchers to remove the corpses that
were now here, walking, in the procession of the forgotten dead.

Many unfamiliar faces passed by. Until he recognized more.
They were those of Crime Hill. They were in the second pile of
corpses he ever saw. The armed men had positioned themselves at
the top of the canyon above Lagunilla River and waited there for the
people on their way to Sunday market. And then when they arrived,

they cut off their heads. And they shaved off one woman's long hair and sent her back naked so she could tell everyone what was happening on Crime Hill. And that was when, that afternoon on his way to school, he saw the mule train carrying the decapitated bodies.

They also disappeared in the distance, silent, those of Crime Hill. Then he briefly caught a glimpse of the fourteen policemen and the captain who died in the assault of Padilla, and he also saw Don Moisés, the shopkeeper decapitated along with thirty-two others who were traveling in a bus to Santa Isabel.

He saw them and countless others and he identified them one by one in his mind, and he remained there immobile, under the Saman tree, in front of the endless throng of lights that advanced without respite toward the horizon. Like the river overflowing its banks, he thought, during the flood of the previous day.

The Aroma of Death

Heriberto Fiorillo

"Arcesio's house smells like a corpse," says Officer Mendoza upon his return to Cascajal at daybreak. It's the end of his beat. He has surveyed the outskirts of town and crossed the plaza to the snack-food stand on the corner.

Inside the aluminum stand, the woman seems to recognize the voice but doesn't bother to turn around and look; she finishes removing the eggs she has been cooking in a pot.

The sentence, accented with the inflections of the Andes Mountains, is not meant for her. A couple of feet away, sitting on the curb, his back resting against a ceiba tree, his body a green mass curled up by the stove, Inspector Santos dozes.

"I'm telling you the place smells like a corpse," repeats Officer Mendoza, craning his neck in search of the inspector's face behind the ample frame of the woman. "I was just there and I had to breathe in that rotten air."

The inspector mumbles under the cap that covers his nose, as if to indicate that he has heard everything the officer said. It is already Friday and the night will soon dispel its darkness between the rooftops of the houses. Mariachi music can still be heard from the bar across the street, as well as the haggard falsettos of a few customers. Church bells announce the early morning mass.

The policeman seizes one of the eggs the woman has placed on the pewter tray next to the coffee cups and glasses of orange juice, peels it, and then dips it into the tin of salt.

The inspector follows the trajectory of the naked, salted egg entering and disappearing into the officer's mouth.

"It's probably an animal they killed and never buried," the inspector says indifferently, returning from his sleepy fog. Then he pulls his cap down straight over his forehead and observes the rhythmic movements of the woman who is fanning the coals with the lid of a pot. She looks majestic on her wooden chair, exuberant and fatigued like a giant carnival figure.

In the background, several shadows in long skirts hastily make their way to the church, avoiding running into other quivering shadows emerging from the bar heading in the opposite direction.

"Dead animals smell different," drawls the officer, before introducing another whole egg into his mouth.

Inspector Santos stands up, brushes the dust from his pants, and lifts his cartridge belt up to his waist. The woman dips a cup into the pot of coffee and hands it to him steaming. The inspector drinks it immediately, face jutted forward, in long, intense sips, his lips stretched out and blowing on it at the same time.

"What I don't understand is how Arcesio and his wife can sleep with that stench," exclaims the officer, who is now leaning on one knee and meticulously cleaning his boots with an orange peel. The inspector detects curiosity flickering in the woman's eyes.

"Let's go, Mendoza," he says quickly. "Let's go and ask Arcesio himself."

The morning slowly begins to fill with its usual disposition. The two men mingle with the shadows in the plaza, turn left at the church, and continue on for two blocks along a stone sidewalk until they reach the vast yellow Olympia movie theater where the back wall functions inside as the projection screen and also marks the end of the town and the beginning of the hill. There, the sandy street ends at a wall of tangled wild thicket and the sidewalk dissolves into a narrow path that plunges into the sea miles below. Halfway down this path is Arcesio's house, on a small farm surrounded by a barbed wire fence.

The inspector stops in front of the theater and observes the faded movie poster.

"They've been showing this same movie forever," he says, discouraged. The policeman is just crossing the street behind him and doesn't hear what he has said.

"Henry Fonda has killed Anthony Quinn in this theater at least five hundred times," adds the inspector, fascinated by the beauty of the images on the poster.

The policeman arrives at his side, looks at the poster, and smiles at the inspector uncomprehendingly but does not shy away from making his own observations.

"Quinn has got to be like the worst bad guy," is what he says. "He and his men lose in every movie."

In the frozen time of the poster, at the end of a long, sandy street, Henry Fonda's slim, elongated shadow fearlessly replaces his smoking gun in its holster, while Quinn's body falls in front of the inspector's eyes, once again and forevermore onto the inert ink of his own blood.

"Here, death is the solution," remarks the inspector, without taking his eyes off the poster. "Otherwise, the movie would never end."

The military man inspects the scene again from top to bottom, reads the small print of the notice, and turns to the minor characters' credits, sensing that the officer has also been reading, with difficulty, over his left shoulder. Then he leans a bit to his right and asks, "And how would you like to die, Mendoza?"

The policeman stops reading but does not appear surprised.

"In my bed, nice and peacefully," he responds casually, almost automatically. But he has caught a glimpse of something, perhaps a vague shadow of disbelief, in the inspector's face, because he quickly adds, in a spontaneous leap to self-defense, "Policemen have a right to dream too, you know. Why don't you ask me how I want to live?"

The inspector does not try to hide his smile.

"How would you like to live?" he concedes, playing along.

The policeman stares down at the tips of his boots, still at attention, and then proceeds to search the infinite sky. When a second later he returns his attention to the eyes of the inspector, the policeman appears just as confident and happy as his answer.

"In a house surrounded by trees, with a swimming pool full of beer."

The inspector looks him up and down. A certain indelible redness appears in the cheeks of the officer—recently arrived from the capital—which always gives away people from the Andes. He observes his fuzz of ringlets holding his hat behind his ears, the metallic shine of the badge on his drill uniform, his shotgun pointing downward, and the damp black of his boots, one shinier with orange peel than the other.

"You're on the wrong side," the inspector says compassionately. "You're in the wrong profession."

"That depends," the officer replies. "I know policemen with Mercedes Benzes."

The inspector lowers his head in reflection.

"Generals . . . ," the inspector specifies, as the officer ventures enthusiastically into the intricate labyrinth of controversy. "You're a sergeant," he reminds him. "You must at least have a little car, or something."

The inspector again contemplates the drawing of Anthony Quinn collapsed on the motionless blood of the poster town.

"I don't have a thing to my name," the officer says and resumes his walk toward the thicket.

A sun-filled sky descends upon them and dampens their backs with its sticky heat, and behind them—far beyond the officer who lags behind the inspector, following his footprints between the mounds of sand and the garbage—the first sounds of morning in the town are fading. They pass the soccer field covered with dry weeds where the children kick around a tattered rag ball in the afternoons, and go into the cemetery with its open vaults and cows that wander around aimlessly eating the flowers on the graves and dispelling dreams and flies.

When they reach the end of the cemetery, the inspector suddenly realizes that the officer has been anxiously speaking to him about Arcesio.

". . . I have a feeling that he's mixed up in something serious," he hears him say. "I haven't seen him since the holidays. He's never been away from Cascajal for so long. Maybe people will take advantage and make problems. . . ."

The inspector perceives a jumble of hopes and fears in the officer's words.

"Are you afraid of him too, Mendoza?" he asks and stops for a moment to give way to a woman in black who is placing tufts of grass and bunches of flowers onto a long row of graves that the windblown sand has deprived of names. When she reaches him, she deposits the last of her offerings on an unmarked grave, murmuring, "Just in case," conjuring unpleasant memories for the inspector.

"Me?" exclaims the emboldened officer. "If I catch him in something, I'll throw him in jail."

The inspector smiles widely, unbuttons the top of his shirt, and fans his neck with his cap. The officer watches him walk off of the path and stop underneath the shade of an immense tamarind tree amongst the scorching aridity of the landscape. He gestures to the officer to come and join him as he sits on an abandoned tree trunk. The officer takes a handkerchief out of his back pocket, places it on another log, and sits facing the inspector, who does not look at him like a subordinate but rather as though the officer were a patient, epitomizing the calm disposition of a veteran physician faced with the inescapable duty of presenting his patient with a painful and prolonged medical report.

"It took me a long time and then some to understand, Mendoza, that the jail in this town was not made for guys like Arcesio Morales.

"The first time we put him in jail, I was the officer who assisted Inspector Acosta, the inspector at that time.

"That day we put him behind bars he was delighted, full of himself the whole time, calling me 'little soldier boy' and waving like a beauty queen to the onlookers who pushed against each other for a glimpse of him from the door to the police station. He told them that he was just planning on spending the night there and that he'd be leaving first thing in the morning at the latest.

"The thing is, Arcesio's behavior was so absurd from the very beginning that I admit having had to stifle my laughter more than once, reluctant as I was to believe there was any truth whatsoever in all of his exaggerated displays of a self-aggrandizing rookie. The undeniable facts that eventually emerged would end up proving, without a shadow of a doubt, just how wrong I was.

"The entire town had witnessed him raiding the Chinese shop that afternoon, destroying their display cases and seriously wounding one of the owners. Not just based on my own moral judgment or my still-intact common sense, but also according to the criminal code, which I, just out of the academy, had learned by heart, Arcesio should have been locked up for at least a few months. The police report stated 'assault with a deadly weapon, personal injuries, property damage, and extortion,' as Inspector Acosta had dictated to his superior via telephone.

"But that's not how it happened. In that particular case, the Chinese victims of the assault never filed a complaint, and they sold the shop and moved to another town. And for Arcesio that incident marked the beginning of an endless series of comings and goings, in and out of jail, detained by us but protected by the silence of the victims and the sway of Don Chema, who had gradually appropriated all of Cascajal and in Cascajal, everybody.

"So at that point, it didn't take me long to realize that a simple threat, a considerable sum of money, a curt phone call from headquarters, or all of these combined, possessed the indiscreet and effectual power of guaranteeing Arcesio Morales' impunity time and time again.

"He vaunted himself and commanded respect everywhere he went as 'Don Chema's right-hand man,' Don Chema being the overlord who had witnessed his birth and his upbringing amongst the duties of his domestic servants and who, when Arcesio had become an adult, made him overseer of the farm laborers. The same Don Chema who had bought, by manifest destiny and for the price of an egg, the Chinese shop.

"According to his admirers, Don Chema Fontalvo was the personification of progress in Cascajal. Everything the town sowed— yucca, sesame, corn, yams, or arracacha root, for example—Don Chema bought. Cheap, but he bought it. Then he had it loaded onto his company trucks and transported to the markets in the city where it was sold.

"The trucks returned loaded with the astonishing comforts of modernity and technology: rolls of toilet paper, cold cuts wrapped in plastic, razors you only use once, beer in cans, and milk in bags. Only Don Chema brought them these things. His prices were a little high, but he brought them.

"With time, it didn't seem at all absurd to anyone that things should have gone so, as they say, splendidly well for Don Chema. So well in fact that in just a few years he had transformed the limits of Cascajal into those of his own estate, even though it ultimately became, they say, too small for him anyway. So he moved to the city, where he continued to reign and make his presence felt thanks to his trucks and to Arcesio who, through his own merits, was promoted and began to perform additional duties with great efficiency.

"For example, if a peasant sowed something that Don Chema had not approved, Arcesio would set fire to his crops. Or if a shop owner bought factory direct instead of from Don Chema's stock, Arcesio would confiscate his wares or throw them into the river. When it came to revenge, he always provided personalized service. He loved to take care of everything himself, from the smallest to the most extreme acts of disobedience to Don Chema, and he did everything in his power, as he put it, to maintain order in the town.

"And I began to realize that Arcesio, although on Don Chema's side, was like me, a kind of policeman. And, as I came to understand, much more than a policeman, because sometimes he was also an implacable judge and summary executioner, without the requirements or restrictions, or the paperwork or precision, that these two occupations require when performed in accordance with the law. According to our law, I should say, because as for Don Chema's law, well, he knew how to apply it quietly but in his own way.

"Arrogant, that Arcesio; he even gave speeches, which in a town like Cascajal—where there are no politicians because all dreams are sown, cultivated, and harvested by Don Chema and where on election day he himself takes families to vote in his trucks—is really gratuitous.

"'You know what?' he said to Inspector Acosta that last night he and I arrested him and put him in jail. 'You're behind the times!'

The inspector didn't pay any attention to him, but he kept berating us, from inside the bars of his cell: 'Everyone here is behind the times! You refuse to accept development and civilization. How many more times are you going to arrest me? Don't hold up progress, Inspector. Times change and so do laws!'

"Two hours later the inspector received the phone call from headquarters, which we had been expecting. Fed up, humiliated down to his core, the inspector stood waiting for the order to wind its way from the other end of the line and coil brutally into his ears. Then he hung up the phone, took his hat from the hat stand, walked to the door where I was hiding my shame among the shadows of the night, gave me the bunch of keys he had taken out of his desk drawer, and said, 'Santos, you know what you have to do. I'm leaving. I quit. This is no place for me.'

"I tried to change his mind; I attempted a few phrases but he remained firm.

"'No, Santos. Let me go now while I still have the courage. In the end, Arcesio is right: times change and so do laws. . . .'

"And he disappeared into the shadows of the night forever.

"So I took on Inspector Acosta's role and then his rank and as such I continued opening and closing and opening the cell door to Arcesio Morales, who was fulfilling his sundry duties with such efficiency and precision that on occasion it seemed to me that I was contending with not one, but many, Arcesios and that it wasn't him but me who was the outlaw.

"Until Tuesday afternoon, when we caught him throwing those two Indians into a ditch by the side of the road, and we brought him in to the station amongst all the shooting and the commotion of the holidays, but this time no one came to get a look at him. That same afternoon, as I was removing his handcuffs and putting him in the cell, he leaned into my face, enveloping me with his breath of sewer water, and said, accentuating each word with the tone and arrogance of a coronal, 'It'll take longer for you to shut this cell door than for me to get out of here, little soldier boy. . . .'

"I received the call from headquarters early, at quarter to seven at night, half an hour before I had expected. Fortunately it came early, because I thought I might lose my mind. The thing is, for some time I had become accustomed to mentally betting on the exact time when I would receive the call. I estimated the time it would take the informant to convey Arcesio's arrest to Don Chema's people, and then how long it would take the request to let him go to reach, through accomplices and secretaries, the commanding officer in the city, and from there the time it would take the official counterorder to reach the police station here. Maybe it was because Don Chema was in town that night—or perhaps because the process of freeing Arcesio, repeated so many times, had become so routine—but the fact is that this time they had been quicker than ever. As incredible as it may sound, just because a system is corrupt doesn't preclude it from aspiring to the glory of perfection.

"'Like I said, little soldier boy. . . ,' Arcesio Morales mumbled as he left, his voice cynical and biting in my ears. Those were his last words."

A gust of wind brings to the inspector's nose the smell of decay that moments before had embedded itself in officer Mendoza's head. He stands up and returns to the path through the thicket, followed by the officer, who has taken some time first to return to reality and then to pick up his shotgun.

The inspector arrives at a fork in the road, takes the path to the right, walks along the barbed wire fence that borders Arcesio's estate, and pushes the zinc gate, which opens wide.

Still behind the inspector, the officer quickens his pace and advances, backward now, with his shotgun poised, covering his boss's back.

The inspector stops in front of the white house with its mud walls and red roof.

"Please, stay here by the door," he tells the officer as he softly but firmly pushes open the wooden door, which gives way easily.

The sun enters the room, tossing the inspector's elongated shadow onto the floor, bathing with its burning radiance the silent solitude of the objects, the wicker furniture, the pink crystal lamp, the portrait of Gardel hanging on the wall, the Chinese porcelain horses on the coffee table.

The inspector removes his hat and walks resolutely toward the room to the right on the other side of the living room. In the bedroom is an enormous skylight through which a stream of light filters and illumines the bare mattress on the bed, stained with blood. It's a rectangular skylight—formed by the absence of several roof tiles—through which a man's body could easily fit. The blood on the mattress is dry, as if it had been there, exposed to the sun, for several hours. But the blood on the floor and walls of the room has been washed, no doubt, with less success than intention.

The room, in which the smell of decay mingles with that of disinfectant, also contains a wardrobe made of wood, a night table, a painting of the Sacred Heart, and a calendar with a half-naked woman on the wall.

He suddenly hears a noise that seems to come from the other end of the corridor. The inspector retraces his steps and is again immersed in the shadows of the house, with all of its windows and doors closed, asking who is there, squeezing the butt of his holstered gun with his right hand, unlatching bolts, and peering into all of the corners until he reaches the door to the kitchen.

Then he covers his nose with his cap, takes a deep breath, opens the door with one push, and faces Arcesio's wife, who, bent over a cutting board and under the tenuous light sifting through the latticework, dices a row of onions next to the sink.

The inspector takes a step forward and the woman backs up against the wall, lowering her eyes. Her name is Inés; she's still very young, she's dressed in black, and her hair is pulled back into a bun. In the fleeting moment in which the inspector manages to catch her eye, he sees a tiny version of himself deep inside the mirror of her sparkling, onyx-like black eyes. But now she buries them once again in the onions.

Asphyxiated by the stench and the heat, they both sweat profusely.

"Do you remember me?" he asks, not so much out of politeness but to make sure.

The woman does not answer.

The inspector has known her for a long time; she was always meticulous and demure, transporting bundles and messages like a maid until she turned twelve and Don Chema snatched her away from her mother's arms and gave her to Arcesio as a wife during a party that in Cascajal came to be known as unforgettable because there was even a piñata with ice cream and chicken stew and *vallenato* music. He would later get used to seeing her arrive, silent and docile, at the jail, each night at dinnertime, when she had to bring Arcesio his meal.

The inspector puts his thoughts aside and fans his neck with his cap.

"Where is Arcesio?" he asks.

The woman takes her time in answering.

"He's on the patio," she says finally, without taking her eyes off the onions but pointing to the large double doors between which the midday sun filters.

The inspector turns on his heels, puts his cap back on his head, and with both hands pulls open the two doors that squeak on their hinges and provoke a feverish fluttering of wings at the far end of the patio. An explosion of light violently bursts into the kitchen, blanching everything and causing the inspector's whole face to wrinkle into an indefinable grimace.

Having overcome the initial shock, the inspector ventures out into the heavy atmosphere of the patio with its lugubrious air. Disturbed by the noise of the opening of the doors, several vultures have gone to perch on the clothesline. The woman in the kitchen is now at the door, behind the inspector, who looks around uneasily.

"Where?" insists the policeman, trying to locate the exact spot.

"There," she points languidly, extending her hand. "Between the cistern and the medlar tree. You'll find him under that pile of dirt."

The inspector notices the shovel leaning against the tree.

"So you killed him and buried him here in the patio," he says with inappropriate flippancy, toning down his nervousness with the weak but flat tenor of a joke.

The woman is now standing in front of the inspector and looks at him with compassion.

"I buried him but I didn't kill him," she points out, investing the sentence with an inflection of honesty that leaves no room for doubt.

The inspector picks up the shovel and sinks it into the mound of loose dirt that the woman had previously indicated to him.

"Then who did kill him?" says the inspector, following the logic of the conversation but taking a wild risk, as he bends down to repeatedly thrust the shovel into the ground.

"It could have been anyone," replies the woman, holding his gaze.

The inspector sighs with relief and begins to feel Arcesio's swollen cadaver underneath the blade of the shovel.

"It smells horrible," he says, wincing. "I don't know how you can stand it."

"I could stand him," replies the woman, who looks up at the high branches of the medlar tree as if searching for fruit.

The inspector repositions the shovel in his hands and uses it as a rake, scraping and sweeping off the dirt that now begins to reveal the contours of the cadaver.

"He's gotten fat . . . ," he remarks.

Indeed, from the woman's improvised grave neatly appear, as if formed in molten rock, the fermented remains of Arcesio Morales, on which it is difficult to distinguish between the wounds from the knife blows and the ulcers from the carrion. The blow to his neck, in just the right place, impelled further by the momentum of the knife's plunge from the skylight, had been enough to kill him.

"They killed him like a pig," says the woman, observing the cadaver and then the inspector with infinite compassion.

The inspector feels no remorse whatsoever. What he has done has simply been a matter of justice. He gets down on his knees and slips his arms under the deceased's head, trying to grab his shoulders in order to lift him up, but then he suddenly removes them. He has just realized, bewildered, that this taking and bringing Arcesio from one place to another appears to have no end.

"Agent Mendoza!" he yells, disconcerted. "Help me get this guy out of here!"

Bitter Sorrows

Darío Ruiz Gómez

The girl appeared to be afraid. She hesitated for a moment—not sure, it seemed, which way to go. But then she reached down, picked up the small suitcase by her side, and crossed the street. The truck was still there. From the back of the truck a man handed bundles down to another man on the street; both of them smiled at her and one of them started to whistle, but the girl seemed to be indifferent to them and to the roguish smile of a well-dressed man in a white jacket standing at the door to a café. Probably a doctor.

The girl stopped when she reached the corner. Instead of crossing the street, she turned left. She started to walk up a rather steep hill. From time to time, the girl coughed. Her skirt was short, rumpled. Probably from sitting for so long. From time to time, too, she stopped and took out a pink handkerchief. Then the girl blew her nose.

She walked up the narrow sidewalk, which was made of small stones in some parts, and in others of brick. And also, here and there, neither of stones nor brick, but simply dirt.

The street was also of cobblestone. Tufts of grass grew in between the stones and right through the middle of the street ran a channel of dirty water. And only the magnified and intermittent sound of the water broke that vast and torturous silence. From time to time the girl stopped, for just a moment, and she rested.

When she arrived at the next corner, she again seemed to be disoriented. Nonetheless, instead of stopping, she crossed the street.

This one wasn't so steep, but it appeared to be more desolate. Ahead was a large lot full of weeds and garbage, nearly spilling out into the sidewalk. The humid air that blew into the girl's face did not bother her very much. Above the rooftops you could see the heaps of passing fog and also, here and there, bits and pieces of mountain. Very few bits and pieces.

The girl carefully observed the doors and windows. But none of them were open. No vestibules in sight. Not a sound came from inside those houses. All of a sudden, a mule appeared. The mule looked at the girl as if surprised to find her emerging from that prevailing silence. But then it went back to nibbling on the grass that grew between the stones on the street.

The mule was too skinny. It barely had what you could call a tail. It looked like a kind of stump, which moved comically back and forth in a vain attempt to shoo away the swarm of flies that hovered over the large wounds on its back.

You could hear the murmur of the water, the liquid prattle, and also the weary snorting of the mule and perhaps some vague and faraway noise. But nothing else could be heard: no voices or distinct sounds.

Then the street was no longer cobblestoned and it turned into a kind of path. There were two houses on the right and three on the left, and then further on, on the right, a mud wall that extended down to a kind of small bridge.

The girl blew her nose. She rested and occasionally looked behind her. But the street was still deserted. Then, when she reached the bridge, she saw a mule, and then another. Then she could see a man whistling, heading toward her. The mules were towing some large planks that, as they dragged along the fine sand, produced a dull and continuous noise.

The girl stepped to the side. The man stopped whistling and when he reached the spot where the girl stood, he removed his hat and greeted her.

"Hey, is this the way to the 'Barrio'?"

The man raised his eyebrows and emitted a guttural sound. Then

he said, "Yeah, just around the corner there. Right after the cemetery," he pointed. "Then you'll see the houses."

The man lifted his hat again as he continued on his way, and
every so often he looked over his shoulder. The girl, when she
reached the cemetery, stopped for a moment. A kind of path led up
to a dilapidated wooden door. On the other side of the path you
could see the walls of a ramshackle house and a few simple wooden
crosses.

The girl walked up to the house and looked around. Fragments
of plates and a piece of something that might have been a chair were
scattered among the grass, and also pieces of burnt wood, papers,
and broken roof tiles.

But there wasn't much left. Even the stone fence that formed a
kind of corral to the left of the house was in bad shape. It was caved
in here and there, as if someone had been kicking it. The girl walked
back to the path. Some cows were grazing ahead. Farther on, an
enormous ceiba tree appeared whose roots extended—like powerful
tentacles—into the path itself.

And farther still, she finally caught sight of a row of houses. But
there were no more than five on each side of what must have been
considered a street. When she reached the first houses, she started to
hear the murmur of a weary tune. A record was playing somewhere
on that peculiar little street. On one side, on the sidewalk, a group of
women chatted gaily.

Leaning against the wall while seated on a stool, a thin, dark man
seemed to dominate the conversation. When the girl approached,
everyone began to stare at her. The women had a sleepy air about
them; with their unpainted faces and uncombed hair, under that
grayish light they looked like sickly figures. The man stopped speaking. He also started to stare at the girl.

The girl put down her suitcase and smoothed down her skirt
to no avail. She stood out sharply among the other women despite
her equally crumpled skirt and cheap shoes. And her yellow socks
clashed with her bright pink skirt and white sandals. But she looked
different.

"What can I do for you, honey?"

"Juaco," said the girl, "I'm looking for Juaco's bar."

"Right across the street."

Almost all the houses looked exactly alike. The one the man had pointed to differed from the others due to its bright blue façade. It had a sign that read "The Last Drink." The girl crossed the street and went into the bar. She entered "The Last Drink."

There was no one there. The shelves, even the bar, were full of beer bottles. A strange shadow hovered above the silent and new jukebox. Above, converging on a kind of lamp that hung from the center of the ceiling, were chains of streamers of different colors and two or three paper lanterns, full of dust. Behind that you could see a door that must have led to a patio or corridor.

The locale was not very large. There were still some bottles on the tables as if the previous night's activity had only just ended. And the floor was littered with mud and dust and empty packs of cigarettes and cigarette butts. And you could see footprints, dragged along the floor.

Next to the jukebox hung a painting of a naked woman. The painting, with the gray light of day, the light that faintly touched it, seemed to come to life. There were posters as well, also of naked women and of women in bathing suits. A notice next to the bar insisted, "He who sells on credit has gone out to collect."

The girl went up to the bar and peered behind it. Then, she picked up her suitcase and went through the back door. Before her eyes appeared a spacious dirt patio, in the center of which you could see a kind of washing trough, a large block of cement. And beyond it was a low wall that also had a door. But the girl had not noticed the dog and only after hearing its howl of pain when she stepped on it did she see it was lying there in the corridor.

The corridor was L-shaped. To the left, lying in the far corner, was another dog. Smoke emerged from the roof of the lean-to, and then a woman's voice began to sing a tune.

The kitchen was full of smoke. The dog lifted its head and growled, but the girl started to call out. Then, as if materializing from the smoke itself, a woman appeared. It must have been the one who had been singing, because she could no longer hear the tune. She was squeezing a mound of corn dough in her hands and turning it over and over. Her eyes were watery.

"What do you want?"

"I'm looking for Juaco. I wrote to him about a month ago and he wrote back telling me to come."

"So? He's not in the bar, or what?"

"No, there was no one there."

"Damn him! One of these days that idiot is going to ruin us. They'll leave us without a cent."

The woman walked down the corridor toward the bar and yelled, "Juaco! Juaco!"

She went into the bar and then out into the street. The women and the man were still sitting across the street. The women said in unison, "He's not here."

"That damn fool! What an idiot!"

The girl followed the woman. The two dogs did as well. Two large, old dogs. The woman went up to the bar and opened a box. Then she looked at the shelves and the paintings and the jukebox and the walls and the streamers.

And she looked at them again. She looked everything over as if to inventory them. The girl had placed her suitcase on one of the tables and had sat on a stool. The dogs were sniffing her now.

The girl removed her headscarf. Her hair was blonde. The curls that fell onto her forehead gave her an air of innocence. She started to yawn and to push away the dogs that were licking her knees. From time to time she coughed.

The woman was still fuming. She paced back and forth from the front door to the back door, calling at the top of her lungs. But the girl's face was impassive. She had lit a cigarette and was inhaling with pleasure.

The man appeared in the front doorway as the woman had her back to him, calling out to the patio. And the woman turned around slowly but when she saw the man her look of fury transformed into a gesture of resignation. He was a rather old man. The girl did not get up from her seat.

"But they were keeping an eye on the place. We're not going to get robbed." Then he said, looking at the girl, "Are you Mariela? I figured as much."

The girl nodded. The gray sky was a changing mass of clusters of fog. The air was filled with a cold and penetrating moisture that stuck to everything with a strange force. Out on the patio everything seemed to ooze with moisture, the peeling-back wall and the washing trough as well. Along the corridor were several withered bunches of geraniums, and, in the eastern corner, a dilapidated urinal of blue and white tiles placed any which way. On the wall was a row of color prints and two empty cages. The girl now smoked indifferently.

The smoke rising from the stove dispersed around the kitchen. The fire crackled. Above, the ceiling was covered with glistening soot. Almost in the center of the room was a small table without a tablecloth. On one side was an enormous box and two small stools. Next to the stove was a large pile of kindling.

The woman continued with her work. Along with two pots there was a gridiron. The woman placed the corn *arepas* on top and then she turned them over. She browned them one by one. And the dogs watched as if wanting to understand something.

The man had sat down on one of the little stools. Above his head hung a side of beef from a large beam. He said, "Well, the truth is, I don't understand why it is you've come. Things here are getting worse and worse."

"It's getting worse everywhere. What's gotten into people that they act like this! Who would have thought that things would have turned out this way?"

"That's right, my girl. Because as far as politics is concerned, that stopped being the reason for people to fight like this a long time ago. That's why, like I said, things are getting worse and worse. When people kill just for the sake of killing, like has started to happen in this town, then there's nothing you can do about it."

"In any case, a girl like me can earn a little something, right?"

"Yeah, that much is true. Thank God there's still some money to go around. But there have also been a lot of people leaving. You can't imagine what the police are like around here."

"The police I already know all too well," said the girl. "They took away my family. They did away with them all in one fell swoop."

"So far they haven't bothered me. I have a few tricks up my sleeve and I've managed to stay on the sergeant's good side."

"You know what, she doesn't look like a professional, that is, like a . . . ? I mean she's not like the other girls, is she?"

It was the woman. She had stared at the girl as she had spoken.

"Yeah, I noticed. You look like you come from a good family. Was it that bad what happened?"

"Yes," said the girl impassively, as if to indicate that she wanted the subject to be dropped. She was sitting now on a large box and her legs dangled, whereas the man had adopted an ape-like posture. He was far too large for the little stool; his knees jutted upwards, and he looked shrunken.

Then the man said, "There's an empty room over there. The girl who was there before left only a week ago. She went off with a policeman who had been transferred to another town."

"Well, at the end of the day, that was the best thing that could have happened to her."

The woman had placed a cup of hot chocolate on the table with an *arepa* and a piece of cheese. The man inched the little stool up to the table, picked up the plate, and put it on his lap.

"There, the second door. Fix it up as best you can and then come and get something to eat."

The girl took a look around the patio. The clucking of the hens was tiresome. A pair of blackbirds hopped about on top of the washing trough. The girl opened the door to the room and put her suitcase down inside. There was a strong smell of dankness. A heavy smell of earth covered everything. Then she turned on the light and a weak glow illumined the room.

Inside the air was heavy; it seemed as if every inch of wood in the room was in the process of rotting. There was a cot made of sackcloth and a clothes cupboard. There was only one pillow—red, without a pillowcase—and a couple of folded bedspreads, green, frayed, placed on the end of the cot. There was also a washbasin, in poor condition, and a pitcher. On the wall, for some unknown reason, were tacked some newspaper clippings. She crouched and looked underneath the cot. Then she lit a match and brought it toward a candle stump that was next to a statuette of the Virgin.

The moisture that covered the bedspreads was sticky. The heavy smell of rot seemed to increase with each passing moment. The cupboard had only two drawers.

She opened the drawers and looked inside. But there was nothing there except a hairpin and a cigarette butt. The girl put the clothing she had in her suitcase into the drawers. She placed a mirror on top of the clothes cupboard, and she looked at herself. She opened her mouth and inspected her tongue. Then she combed her hair. Then she cried.

She was woken up by the noise of people and music. Sometimes it was a languid rhythm that prevailed above all of the others but then all you could hear was a raucous melody. The place, that little street, tucked into the night, looked even smaller than it really was. The five houses in front, and the other five, all with their weak light bulbs and rudimentary signs: "The Coquito Bar," "The Farewell My Love," etc. Those little houses at night looked just like mangers.

The girl looked up at the sky, the brightness of the moon above the vast clouds, and the dark patch of the mountain peak that looked as if it were sitting right on top of the street. Like a sleeping giant.

The girl went into the bar and sat down on a stool next to the jukebox, where a row of stools had been placed. Five stools. But the girl said nothing. There were three women: two on her left and one on her right.

There was also a group of men, the only customers, drinking raucously. A man and woman danced. The men looked at the couple and then broke into laughter. And the woman who was dancing also laughed. When they looked at her, she opened her mouth and made faces. She was wearing a shimmering purple dress, and her flesh jiggled as she moved. You could see her brown thighs and razor bumps on her legs.

The place was poorly lit. There was an opaque glow that did not manage to prevail over all of the shadows. The couple continued to dance. The girl coughed but her face remained impassive. Behind the bar, the old man opened bottle after bottle. You could hear the muted sound of caps popping off and then the woman came and she placed the bottles on the tables.

The laughs of those men were so powerful sometimes that they drowned out the languid trail of the music from the jukebox. The barman's wife shook off anyone who tried to grab her hips. Then the woman went up to the girl.

"So, why don't you go on over and sit with them," she said with her cloying voice. "Looks like they're loaded."

"I don't want to sit with those fools. Do me a favor and play 'Bitter Sorrows.'"

The woman couldn't hide her chagrin. The other women smiled, watching the group of men drink. The couple stopped dancing and sat down. The woman sat on her companion's lap and put her arm around his shoulder. And the rest gossiped amongst themselves in loud voices. The place reeked of beer, sweat, and humidity. And from the street, every so often, a cold, harsh wind blew in that tossed the streamers and the lanterns.

Passersby came and watched from the door. They stood there with amused looks on their faces as they watched the women. They pressed against each other and when the women began to shout insults, they smiled and slowly withdrew. Some didn't seem to pay attention to what was being said to them. Some even responded disdainfully or maliciously. But the light continued to flicker. It was getting more and more scandalously weak.

The damp floor already reflected an infinite number of arabesques, tracks left behind by the dancers and the women in their languorous passage from one end of the locale to the other. The girl drank slowly, removed, it seemed, from all that surrounded her; she was certainly indifferent to that brazen battle between women and onlookers.

The whirr of the jukebox, the muted sound of the motor, could be heard above the music—that sound like rusty hinges—and the record turned slowly, in fewer revolutions than was called for. And the thick voice of the singer was such that he, or she, sounded utterly worn out. The girl hummed softly, barely moving her lips, painted purple.

The other women continued with their insults. The women gestured vulgarly; sitting there they all looked alike, ageless, with their gaudy and tight-fitting dresses, revealing their knees. They leaned back on their stools against the wall. You could hear the men laughing outside, their stares insistent. You could see them among the shadows, moving their hats.

That woman had put her companion's yellow hat on and was still sitting on his lap. He now appeared less jovial. As did the other men, who occasionally turned around to look at the girl but didn't say anything. Not a word. They watched her in silence.

"They're just a bunch of kids. Those guys, they don't have a cent to their name," said a fat woman, barefoot, with a rosy face. She had been sitting next to the girl the whole time but had never turned to look at her even once, nor had she tried to speak to her.

Then the girl smiled. She lifted the bottle and drank in large gulps. Suddenly, the onlookers dispersed from the doorway and the jukebox stopped. The murmur of the night, the sonata of crickets, could be heard like a faraway but distinct chorus.

The girl walked up to the door and it was then that she saw the policeman. The policeman who, there in the middle of the street, was affectionately slapping his horse's rump. Then the girl said, "Well, finally, the police. The officers have finally arrived."

You could sense the powerful smell of the policeman, a combination of man and animal sweat. He wasn't wearing chaps so his boots, as well as most of his pant legs, seeped water and mud.

His horse was also sweaty. The policeman loosened the saddle's girth and then entered the bar, his spurs clanking against the cement floor. His hat, sitting askew on his head, revealed a tuft of damp hair.

He started to remove his spurs without taking his eyes off the girl. She was still standing in the doorway. She had followed the policeman's movements only with her eyes. And she was smiling. The men who were sitting at the table, in front of the policeman, remained silent. As did the woman on the man's lap, now completely drunk. Half asleep.

There was less noise now. The fog entered the bar. The gray masses were carried inside in waves by the wind. The light was getting fainter. The girl walked up to the bar but without looking at the policeman. She stopped in front of the jukebox. But then the policeman appeared next to her, smiling, now without his spurs, which he had left next to the stool. The policeman said, "I like 'Bitter Sorrows.'"

"Really? Looks like I got myself a clever one."

The girl brushed her finger along the policeman's chin. The other women had stopped talking as well. They seemed to be asleep. But they continued to show off their pitiable knees. And the four men drank in silence, looking at each other. The music stridently inundated the bar.

"Come and sit with me," said the policeman.

There was no one left at the door. The barman's wife emerged from behind the bar and placed a bottle of beer on the table, smiling at the policeman. The policeman poured a little beer into his glass and then poured it out onto the floor. The other men watched attentively. It was cold. The policeman drank a whole glass of beer in one gulp. His voice was disjointed and his breathing hard. The girl drank as well, observing him in silence.

"How are things today? A lot of work?"

The policeman rubbed his chin, wiping off the sweat and the damp mist of the night. His face exuded a strange grimace.

"Today we gave those people all the firepower they wanted."

He pulled up the sleeve of his jacket and revealed a small wound.

"One of them almost got me. But you should've seen how he screamed when we set his house on fire!"

The torpor of the liquor enveloped the policeman completely. But you couldn't tell if those large damp stains were from sweat or rain. He danced, dragging his feet weakly. The girl was almost as tall as him. Even in her sandals. The girl allowed the policeman to squeeze her tight.

At one point he hiked up his jacket, revealing his revolver. He spoke as if in a dream, his words disjointed. And the smell of alcohol and exhaustion hit the girl full in the face.

The music had changed. You could hear an accordion and some maracas. The policeman whooped every so often. He kept lifting his arms and removing his hat. But the girl did not smile. She leaned on the policeman's shoulder. He was an old drinker dancing giddily. He had removed his poncho. And after lifting his arms so often as if in praise, his shirt ended up coming out of his trousers.

From behind the bar, the barman laughed whenever the girl looked at him. The shadows made him look older than he was, like a man suffering from utter exhaustion. He said to the policeman, "Good, isn't she?"

The policeman closed his eyes. He did not answer. He squeezed the girl again, and again he whooped. Later, when the other policemen showed up at the door, his yells got more piercing. He started to greet them in a loud voice. The women seemed to suddenly come back to life. They went up to the door, to the policemen.

There were no longer any onlookers. The old man behind the bar put on a face of false delight. The policeman continued to squeeze the girl; he lifted her up by the waist. He brought the bottle of beer up to her lips and made her drink. The foamy liquid streamed down her slim neck and dampened her pink silk dress, dampened the girl.

In the darkness of the patio, the cold was penetrating. You could hardly see a thing. But the dogs began to growl and you could see their eyes right there and then feel their tongues and wet snouts. The policeman weaved about, leaning on the girl. The candle flickered under the bed.

The girl laid her head against the pillow. Through the cracks in the door entered the music, the shouting, the noise of the crickets, and the barking of the dogs.

You could hear the distinctive sound of clothing dropping to the floor. The policeman's heart was beating fast. You could barely see his face, flat profile, and large hands.

The policeman said nothing. He had leaned his head against the girl's shoulder and you could only hear his quickened breathing and the noises from his stomach.

His hat was on the clothes cupboard, as was his shirt and bayonet. He still wore his revolver; the girl could feel its coldness against her arm. The policeman uttered disjointed words. Sometimes he lifted his arms as if to claw at something.

The girl placed her hand on his sweaty chest and began to whisper things into his ear. The policeman replied with disjointed sentences or words: "We have to kill them all. Their offspring even, they have to go."

The girl again whispered in his ear. The policeman repeated, "Can't leave even the offspring of those bastards." The girl observed his tense neck and brushed her hands along his chest.

The noises had now diminished. You could hardly hear the crickets and, perhaps, a voice here and there. Someone was in the urinal. And he was laughing, under his breath. And you couldn't even hear the barking of the dogs.

The bayonet came out of its sheath with a muted sound. It was not polished. The policeman convulsed violently and his weak moan was barely audible. Then he went limp. The candle had gone out. Abruptly. It had hissed and then gone out. Nothing could be heard now. A heavy silence had fallen. Then, when the girl extended her arm and thrust the bayonet into the floor, she felt the warm and sticky trickle of droplets hitting her hand.

Eme

Julio Paredes

Eme got drunk too fast. She seldom drank so she didn't know how to calculate exactly how much tolerance she had. She had an explosive character and acted as if she always had an excess of accumulated energy. Nonetheless, she was happier than ever that night, and didn't care if she ended up with a terrible hangover the next day. Before going dancing they had cooked a special dinner in their apartment to celebrate Johnny's new job in a well-known construction firm. She loved Johnny. The magnitude of her love for him frightened her, as if measuring it might crush her. And she was happy that night because finally, after almost a year, Johnny had found work.

Her forehead was resting on her sleeping arm, bent feebly on the edge of the table. She didn't want to move. She was afraid that if she lifted her head she would get another attack of dizziness. She was aware that her sister and the two friends they had come with were still talking next to her. Johnny had left the table some time ago and had not returned. She wanted to call out to Johnny but decided it would be better to sleep a little. Sleep until she sobered up. But she couldn't help following the rhythm of the music. How she loved dancing, she thought. Better than sleeping and working, as her lovely Johnny would say when he was in a cheerful mood. Of course, he wasn't much of a dancer and what he really liked to do was sit in front of the stereo and listen to it very carefully, concentrating, as if he wanted to decipher the true and secret meaning behind the harmony. He would hover over the stereo as if he wanted it to swallow him up, although he always ended up being reminded of his frustrated career as a musician. Then Eme would go up to Johnny and hug him and they would laugh. Since they started living together, they rarely allowed themselves to fall into glumness.

She tipped over a bottle with her elbow, and the noise of the shattering glass woke her. She opened her eyes, waited for a moment, and then lifted her head. Her sister was dancing with one of her friends in the small space that served as a dance floor. She looked for Johnny. He was standing at the far end of the small bar talking with a couple of guys. Johnny occasionally raised his arm as if he were giving a speech. Eme saw his profile and thought she noted a look of annoyance on Johnny's face. There was a time before meeting her when Johnny often got into fights. He liked to argue and curse and he routinely lost control. Johnny used to tell Eme how in those days the smallest things would drive him mad, and getting into fights eventually became a kind of hobby for him.

"How are you?" asked the friend still sitting next to her.

"I could use a soda water with lemon and ice."

Her sister came back to the table and asked if she wanted to leave. Eme assured them that she felt better. She lit a cigarette but put it out right away. She looked for Johnny again, but one of the guys he was talking with was blocking her view. She stretched out her legs and felt the need to urinate. She calculated the distance from where she was sitting to the bathroom and doubted she could make it there without falling over a table on the way. She'd wait a little longer until she felt stronger.

She suddenly noticed that a commotion had erupted around Johnny. The people at the bar abruptly stepped back. There was a moment of silence amongst those who had been shouting and then she heard an insult. Eme wasn't sure if it had been Johnny's voice. There was a quick, abrupt movement among the people sitting at the tables near the bar. Eme stood up. She walked toward the bar and saw that a guy had Johnny in a headlock. Johnny was flailing feebly like a deflating rubber doll. For an instant, both of them grunted, motionless, and as soon as the guy loosened his grip, Johnny managed to break free and then give him a powerful kick in the stomach.

Eme tried to get closer but someone pushed her back violently and made her lose her balance. She looked around anxiously for her sister, and when she tried to get up, she heard people screaming in fear and then, all at once, the sound of a gunshot filled the club.

Someone grabbed her arm and dragged her toward the door. She crashed into an incredible tangle of bodies and in the tumult was punched in the mouth and nearly knocked over again. She heard two more shots before making it out into the street. When she got outside, she thought she heard Johnny calling her and she wanted to go back in. She broke free from the hand that was pulling her arm, but then found herself face to face with two guys who were jumping out the door. She recognized her sister's voice yelling for them to get out of there, screeching as if she had fallen into a horrific ambush. Eme obeyed without hesitation, but when she started running, she felt the pavement swelling up beneath her and fell to her knees. The pain made her momentarily lucid again. She understood that she had to act quickly. She let her sister lead her by the hand; they rounded the first corner, rushing in a madcap escape down the middle of the street.

After a while they stopped. Eme painfully swallowed a molasses-like substance that had filled her mouth. She imagined that the last punch had destroyed the roof of her mouth and that it was now dissolving into little pieces. She leaned against a light post and couldn't hold back the vomit. The violent torrent made her tremble and she had to sit down on the curb. Her sister rubbed her back firmly with the palm of her hand. Eme stretched out her legs and carefully examined her stained and ripped pants. She bent her left leg and passed her fingertips over her wounded knee, which protruded from the fabric like a little muddy head.

"Let's wait here for a minute," said her sister, sitting next to Eme.

"Shouldn't we go back?" asked Eme, and she realized that it was starting to rain.

"Jorge and Miguel told us to wait for them."

"What happened to Johnny?" Eme murmured, lowering her head in between her knees. She crossed her arms and tried to control the trembling of her body.

She wanted to understand what had just happened, but the vomit returned like a lightning bolt. She didn't have time to sit up, and stained her pant leg. She was suddenly overcome with disgust and furiously rubbed the soles of her shoes against the pavement. She began to cry, with short, quick spasms that then merged with a renewed bout of retching that forced her to bend over once again.

"A tooth," remarked Eme, catching her breath.

"What?"

"They knocked my tooth out."

"A tooth?"

"Yeah, a lower one. I think I swallowed it."

Her sister didn't say anything.

"What are the lower teeth called?" asked Eme.

"I don't know."

"But what are they called?" Eme nearly shouted.

"I don't know. Same as the upper ones. I don't know, it doesn't matter," her sister replied softly and gently stroked Eme's head. Then she wiped Eme's nose with a handkerchief and Eme realized that her lips were swollen and hot.

A sudden gust of wind scattered the drizzle and seemed to lift the water up to the trees. The street was deserted and for some reason no one else had headed in that same direction. Eme now clearly remembered the scene of Johnny's fight. Damn it, she thought. Johnny had promised her never to fight again, that his days of wandering around the city like a rabid dog—stubborn, raging, churning out that same chaotic rant—had been left behind, forgotten forever like a ruinous love affair. She saw her sister's shadow getting up and asked her what time it was.

"It's two o'clock."

"We can't stay here."

"Jorge and Miguel . . . ," said her sister, eyeing the street corner.

"We have to look for Johnny," said Eme, and she was horrified by the idea that Johnny might be dead.

She shook her head vigorously, as if to hurl that horrific possibility far away. It was a forbidden thought, a speculation she always tried to avoid. What's more, no one had ever explained to her how to accept as natural the irremediable catastrophe of disappearing forever. Neither her parents nor her school nor her friends had prepared her to consider, for even a split second, that the day might come when she would have to accept the fact that from one moment to the next Johnny would not be coming back, submerged and immobile in his abyss. She opened her mouth, gulping air, and asked her sister to help her get up.

"We have to go back," she pleaded, wiping her nose with the back of her hand.

"I don't know," her sister faltered. "It could be dangerous."

"But we have to look for Johnny," repeated Eme, and she started to cry again, silently, controlling the spasms.

They decided to walk along the middle of the street, arm in arm. Eme was surprised by the surrounding calm, as if the incident at the bar had happened somewhere deep underground. She had to stop. She let go of her sister's arm, leaned against a wall, and breathed deeply. She closed her eyes.

"Are you alright?" asked her sister, coming toward her.

She nodded and wiped the cold sweat off her forehead. Her sister stared at the corner and Eme realized that she too was trembling all over, and she thought that at any moment they might pass out and fall flat on their faces.

"What happened?" murmured her sister, still eyeing the corner.

Eme didn't reply. She felt as if her sister's words were coming from very far away. She wiped her eyes with the sleeve of her jacket. The drizzle dissipated little by little until it stopped. Eme crossed her arms and inserted her hands into her armpits to keep warm.

"What time is it?" she asked again.

"A little after two thirty," answered her sister without looking at her watch.

They suddenly heard a siren. They saw a police car two blocks ahead, heading away from the bar. They waited until the wailing completely disappeared, vigilant, motionless, silent.

"Where did everyone go?" remarked her sister. She seemed very scared and unsure of what to do next.

Eme thought of Johnny again and bit her lip. Her throat was parched and she felt the blood rushing violently through her head and she shuddered as if her arms and legs were going to fall off at any moment, scattering along the middle of the street.

"Just when everything was going so well," murmured Eme, looking at her sister.

"What?" she asked, distracted, rubbing her arms and without taking her eyes off the intersection the police car had crossed.

They decided to keep on walking, but when they got to the corner they stopped again. They stood motionless for some time and neither of them seemed inclined to go on. Eme rested her forehead on her sister's shoulder. They stayed like this for several minutes as if posing for a photograph. Eme sighed and suddenly recalled an afternoon a long time ago at her parent's house. She was alone, reading a story about a woman who was waiting anxiously for a phone call from a guy she was very much in love with. A few days earlier the man had promised that he would call her that very afternoon at a specific time. Over two excruciating hours had passed and the telephone still wouldn't ring. The guy had promised her, he had sworn that he would call. The woman had no way of contacting him and started to beg God to please take pity on her and make the phone ring before any more time went by. It was just a trifling request that God should have no problem granting. She'd never ask him for anything again; she would try, if God heard her plea, to mend her ways, to never again commit the sins that had led her astray in the past. She pleaded with him because she was suffering terribly. She vowed to be sweet and understanding toward others, toward her mother and her sister, but please, God, she begged, let the phone ring. God couldn't be cruel and harsh faced with such a trivial, simple request. But time did not stop and the phone did not ring. Would God hear Eme that night? She knew that something horrific happened every night in that damned city—people died and disappeared in the most wretched ways—but Johnny had never been such a bad guy as to end up like that. They had both done the right thing. There were times when others' suffering affected them, but, above all, they wanted to live happy and peaceful lives. Please, God, she begged again, neither of us deserves such pain. God, she continued, pleading in silence, this time is different.

She wanted to get going. She released her sister's arm and began to run. She couldn't understand what her sister was shouting, but she heard her running behind her.

The bar was closed. A few people were talking in low voices across the street. Eme was surprised to find everything so quiet and she wanted to believe that everything that had just happened had been a hallucination, a figment of her imagination that had flashed through her mind to mock her. But snapping out of it, she leapt toward the door and started pounding on it. There was no answer. Her sister was talking with the people across the street. She rested her forehead on the wood and waited. Then she gave the door a feeble kick. How absurd that these things should happen; no one could stand this madness for long. She started to cry. Johnny always said she was a crybaby, that she liked to dramatize everything. But it wasn't true; she only cried when something hurt her, hurt her bad. She was not a crybaby, she thought; on the contrary, she loved to laugh at everything, laugh hysterically.

"They said they don't really know what happened," said her sister. "It looks like the police came and arrested a few people."

Eme pounded the door again with her fist, dismayed by the thought that Johnny could be injured because of her, helpless because she had run off like a madwoman.

"What do we do now?" asked her sister, wiping her face with her hand.

Eme kicked the door furiously until her sister stopped her.

"Relax. We don't know what happened and Jorge and Miguel might come back. Let's wait."

Eme took a deep breath and sat down on the curb, with her back against the door.

"Yes, let's wait. Someone has to come back for us. Johnny must be looking for me," said Eme, calmer now. She touched her swollen lip gingerly and with the tip of her tongue searched for the hole where her tooth used to be.

She would sit still, without moving, for as long as necessary, until Johnny came and warmed her up with a big hug. She would think about something else. About the night that was beginning to clear up. She'd concentrate on the intermittent barking of the dogs, on the water dripping somewhere off to her right. She'd count the seconds between each drop. She'd think about Johnny's new job. She was sure the people there would like Johnny. He was attractive and nice. He read books, he took an interest in world events, he had a sensitive heart. Johnny wanted to get a cat, but the apartment was too small and the animal would probably end up running away. Johnny wanted to travel, to go to places where no one else would even consider going, like Scandinavia or the desert in Brazil. She combed through her damp, disheveled hair with her fingers. Her body started trembling again, more violently than before. Her sister was standing up smoking, carefully blowing out the smoke toward the sky. Yes, she'd sit, still, motionless against the wood like a woman forever trapped inside a painting. Motionless until God let Johnny come back.

The Feast

Policarpo Varón

I wanted to watch the people play pool. Since it was so hot that afternoon, I ordered a glass of ice-cold lemonade and sat down in a corner. Of course, sometimes I had to get up when the onlookers went up to the pool table for the tough shots and blocked my view. I'd crane my neck above them and it was funny ending up right in front of the short player's butt, that guy whose name I can't remember now, who would almost be lying flat on the table. Then the onlookers would go back to their places.

It was at this moment that the man arrived. I had never seen him before. Now I know that his name is Ramón. And he had had one too many *aguardientes* because he came in yelling, causing quite a commotion, and brandishing an empty bottle. Then I said to myself, "It's time to go." But the asshole was heading toward me. "Shit, here we go," I thought. Then the man started: "Have a drink with me, Abelardo," and he grabbed my arm and pushed me over to a table, and then he said, "Come here, I'm paying, it's on me, don't let me down, man."

Well, I played along, but then he just wouldn't let up. "I don't drink," I said, but the man had made up his mind. I kept saying no, he kept saying yes. I decided to slip away and go out to the plaza, but he grabbed me hard. I had to struggle a lot because the man was big. The beers were already on the table. The man picked one up and threw it at my face and then I said, "That I'm not going to take, asshole," and I punched him right in the face, and the guy fell on his ass in the corner with his nose bleeding, and I said to myself, "Now you've really got to split. . . ."

I headed for the door but the police were already advancing through the plaza; scruffy policemen, with their shirts open, just putting on their caps, positioning their rifles on their shoulders and the sergeant in front hurried them along, but those policemen looked really sleepy, and for good reason, because it was the middle of the afternoon when the heat is at its fiercest in San Bernardo de los Vientos, when you can't bear sitting still. And the sergeant turned around and no doubt said, "Move, goddamn it, can't you see there's a fight," and the policemen made like they were hurrying. And when they arrived they almost couldn't get in because of all the people already gathered in the doorway of the café. The policemen had to go in saying, "Make way, make way, for God's sake," and pushing people to either side with the butts of their rifles.

I was closest to the door. The other had just gotten up from the corner and was wiping his nose and his rear end with his shirtsleeve, and that was when the sergeant went up to him (I could swear the sergeant was smiling, mocking the poor guy) and he said to everyone, or looking at everyone but only asking the man and myself, "What's going on here . . . ?" Then the man spoke. He told the sergeant that I had punched him. And that sergeant, impassive, said to me, "You come with us," and he shoved me in the ribs. It wasn't a shove made to keep me by his side; it was a mighty thrust that almost sent me flying into the street. And the policemen surrounded me and took me to the station and everyone was in their doorways whispering, no doubt saying, "They got Abelardo," although I couldn't hear them. . . .

But I did hear when old Empera, who had watched everything from the corridor of her ranch, turned around and went into her house and then, with all of that fervor she always puts into everything she says, she said to her kids or to her husband (Vigilio is the old man's name), "Shit, they got Abelardo. . . ." Empera said it, that old woman with the massive hips, big and raucous; I managed to hear her and everyone else in San Bernardo de los Vientos probably heard her too, because in this town everyone hears everything the old lady says in her house, whether she's yelling at her kids or fighting with the old man, and you can almost feel the clamor of her hips and the wind raised by her petticoat when she goes around the corner to buy a pound of rice or a packet of cumin. . . . And no doubt when they heard her, heard what old Empera had said, everyone came to the conclusion that they had in fact gotten Abelardo, and they went to the plaza and saw how the policemen (actually, only one) removed the ancient door—the thick, steel-green, rusted door without hinges—and didn't open it, but removed it and said, "Go in." And he pointed to that room—full of stones, cockroaches, leaves, shit, and urine—that smelled like hell, and then I had to go in because if not they were going to kick my ass in there, and that policeman—irritable because of the smell—put the door back on its frame, and I didn't see him because I still hadn't noticed the holes the kids had made with stones. I didn't see him when he said, "And don't try to escape, asshole, because we'll break your legs with one shot, that is, if we don't send you to your grave once and for all, got it . . . ?" So I cleared a space for myself next to the door, shoving all the crap to one side with my shoes, and I sat down, and that was when I saw the holes in the door, the holes the kids had made when there weren't any policemen in San Bernardo de los Vientos, and when cows, dogs, pigs, and men passing through town had slept in that room that's now a cell, and where kids had shit at night when they played in the plaza because there weren't any policemen, there wasn't, that is, anyone to restrain them.

I didn't see them until nightfall. The first street lamps had been lit on the corners of San Bernardo de los Vientos. I had spent quite some time allowing the mosquitoes to hum and gather over my head so as to clap my hands and crush a bunch of them together. That's why I hadn't noticed that a crowd of people had gathered in front of the station and that the policemen were standing in the corridor with their rifles cocked. It was dinnertime and I said to myself that no one was going to remember to feed poor Abelardo. But then I heard the first shouts of the people, of the men; I heard some familiar voices—some tenuous, fearful voices, alone at first, then dense, in unison—that cursed the policemen and said, "Let him go, murderers, you're just going to throw him into the river tonight," and things like that, and the policemen, of course, weren't about to keep their mouths shut, and they cursed back at them and they threatened them with their guns and said, "Go home. . . ." But the people just stayed there in front, ignoring them, and the policemen were afraid to shoot because there were so many of them, about a hundred or more, and there were only eight of them and each had only six bullets.

When I began to hear all of this—I mean, when I realized that all these people were in the plaza talking, shouting for me—then I went back up to the holes in the door and let the mosquitoes suck the blood out of my ears, my neck, my throat, and my forehead. I didn't swat at them because now I was watching what was going on in the plaza, although it cost me. . . . Of course, I had to open my eyes wide to be able to see anything and then carefully press my ear against the holes of the door because I couldn't do both things at the same time. . . .

Anyway, the people stopped yelling when they heard the motor of the car approaching along the river. The headlights briefly lit up the throng and then were turned off, and then the motor stopped humming, and you could hear a few doors opening, and everyone turned around to see who that tall, stout, hairy, bespectacled figure was who was coming toward them. "It's the lawyer," I heard. "The lawyer that came down this morning from Ibagué." Now he was going to speak on Abelardo's behalf. Now he was going to get Abelardo out because several townspeople had sent for him and were speaking to him. They waved their arms, they gesticulated a lot, and they no doubt told him about what had happened that afternoon. The lawyer agreed to represent me and went up to the policemen, and they braced themselves, but when they saw that it was the lawyer they lowered their rifles a bit and the lawyer spoke for a few moments with the sergeant, and the sergeant told him that they weren't going to let me go until the following day when the mayor returned from Ibagué. So then the lawyer had no other alternative but to leave and tell the men that there was nothing he could do; by now quite a few onlookers had gathered. . . . Then that lawyer, who had not been able to get me out of jail despite having been offered a fortune, dashed back to his car and got in with his wife and children and swiftly headed for the capital. . . . Soon the sound of the motor disappeared beyond the plains and I thought that I would have to spend the night there in jail, without eating, having to endure that smell of shit and the mosquitoes, and I wasn't at all sure if I'd live through the night. . . .

It was the next day, or maybe a few days later, when the new policemen arrived. They arrived in a gray truck, making a lot of noise, raising a cloud of dust in the plaza, and dispersing the animals that had been scrounging for scraps because the people hadn't moved and so the animals hadn't been fed. . . . At first I didn't believe it, because I had seen the people there in front, I had watched them for a long time, for many hours before falling asleep on the cold, filthy cement, dead tired, fighting against exhaustion, afraid to fall asleep because the police could come for me in the middle of the night and drag me to the river and push me off the bridge and good-bye said the fly, here end the tribulations of Abelardo. . . . Yes, those policemen turned out to be even more dogged than the last ones. They pushed their way through with fixed bayonets and stood at attention between the people and the station. Then the lieutenant, or some guy who commanded them, advanced a few steps, a few meters, and shouted at the people that they had ten minutes to leave, that then there would be a curfew, and that the curfew was going to be a gun shot. But those people, starving, enraged, weren't about to leave and instead they started to tell them off, and again you could hear the curses hurled at the policemen, and the jumping with arms flailing and fists raised; I saw them, yes, as red as faces can be, and Empera lifting her petticoat and shouting insults over her shoulder, and I felt like laughing (although it was no time to laugh) because Empera's insults were very funny, really vulgar, because that old lady was bent on hurling an insult a day and when she showed her face you had better get as far away as you could. It was those shouts that angered the lieutenant or captain and especially the fact that the people began to inch forward, trying to get into the policemen's faces. Those people of San Bernardo de los Vientos: when they get mad, they mean business.

The Feast

I saw from my cell how that lieutenant started to get scared, like he was overcome with terror, like he realized what a dicey situation he was in, and then he shouted at the people that their ten minutes were almost up, that they better leave or he was going to give the order to shoot, and instead of retreating, the people advanced even farther, got closer and closer to the lieutenant and his policemen, and then I said to myself, "This lieutenant isn't as tough as he makes himself out to be," because he was faltering, he had gone fainthearted, he was weak-kneed-shaking-all-over, wanting to turn around and forget about the whole thing. But then he had to say to the policemen, "Give it to them," and the policemen weren't sure how, whether with rifle butts, bayonets, bullets, curses, or shots in the air, and they started to try to make the people retreat but the people didn't take their shoving seriously and they started to hit the policemen as best they could, and then the lieutenant, feeling cornered, said to his policemen, "Shoot," and they just squeezed the triggers the slightest bit with their fingers. . . .

I saw them fall from my cell, with my pair of eyes pressed against the holes in the wood, and the women ran as fast as they could and the children as well, and the policemen advanced in crouching position and didn't stop shooting, and more fell, many while running through the plaza, and others were screaming on their bellies in the dust on the ceiba leaves, on the tamarind and caracoli leaves, and many said, "Ay my head, ay I'm dying, ay my children, ay my stomach, ay my balls, ay my legs."

It broke my heart to see all those people there, some nursing mothers, others expecting, and many children, the poor little kids never having had a chance to really live. But I didn't have the strength to move, my legs wouldn't respond, my whole body was going numb squatting in the cell, and the policemen were already finishing off the ones who were left and searching for those who had escaped, breaking doors, shooting at the animals, those poor animals that had nothing to do with this. . . .

Then I saw the priest, redder than usual, giving last rights to the fallen, sweating; the priest was sweating, moving amongst the dead, touching them with something and praying in a soft voice, and then

I saw him get up and say something to the policemen and the lieutenant, and I heard the lieutenant telling him to go to hell, that is, he
said something that I didn't hear very well, but that sounded like,
"Shut up, Father, and go back to your church," and the priest gathered his petticoats and hastened back to where the lieutenant had
sent him. . . .

The bodies had been lying in the plaza on the dust and leaves for
several days. The color of the bloodstains had changed with the sun.
The corpses had become bloated; they were pale and began to smell.
Then, attracted by the stench, the first buzzards arrived. I had had to
position myself very artfully to be able to see them from the cell.
There were only a few of them circling very high above the town.
But soon more and more of them gathered; they came from all
directions—from the South, from the North, from San Juan, from
Picalá, from Llano Largo—and little by little they began forming a
black cloud that circled down and down, until they alighted on the
roofs of San Bernardo de los Vientos. . . . And at the end of the afternoon, when you can't say for sure if it's day or night, at the evil hour,
as they say, the buzzards slowly began to descend, opening their
wings, making that hideous sound with their beaks as if they were
spitting, or secreting phlegm, dragging their feet along the roofs, the
straw, and the palm leaves. . . . That was when the smell started, the
smell of rotting flesh, that fetid stench of decay, a terrifying smell. . . .
And I said to myself, "Now you're really screwed." And there was
that flapping all night long, that flying from one roof to another,
that swooping and swooping of buzzards. "All of the buzzards of the
earth have come," I thought, and I couldn't take the stink anymore.
And as they couldn't all fit in the trees or on the roofs, they went at
each other with their wings and legs. . . . And in the morning, the
king, the oldest and biggest of the buzzards, descended from the roof
where it had spent the night alone. That buzzard—so old it was almost gray, not all black, with its long, red neck, very red, as if it had
just removed it from a pool of blood—descended alone, and walked
among the bodies, and it stood on top of the bloated bellies and
rubbed its beak in their hair and their faces, and shit its white shit
several times, its shit reeking of rotting flesh, and finally it sat on a

corpse in the center of the plaza and plunged its beak with all of the strength of its neck, steadying itself on the bloated belly with its legs, and it leaned back and ripped the fetid flesh apart, making that noise, that noise that flesh makes when buzzards devour it, that noise that makes you feel the pain in your own flesh, and you can't stand watching it because it hurts you too and makes you nauseated . . . And when that huge buzzard, the king, swallowed a big piece and made a deep hole in that belly, it turned and looked up at the sky and then yes, as if summoned, the other buzzards swooped down on the bodies, the black cloud fell, and the body was just flapping wings, tugs, and pecking. . . .

I was horrified when I saw this and, burying my fear, I pushed open the cell door, which fell to the ground in pieces, and the buzzards, frightened, flew away and watched me from the trees and the roofs stagger across the plaza and head for the river. . . . Then they swooped down on the corpses again and they would no longer be disturbed because no one lived in San Bernardo de los Vientos, and the police had left ages ago. . . .

Vendors of Peculiar Objects

Celso Román

City dweller Pascual Colonia Nemesio tried to sell his little finger on Tenth Avenue. "When you're a street peddler, you have to get up very early to get a space on the sidewalk," he told the journalists who interviewed him at the downtown police station, where he was being held for disturbing the peace.

Before seven in the morning—when the city was just beginning to stir before the daily rush that three hours later transforms it into an agitated swarm, an enraged wasp's nest, or an incredible bustle of activity—Pascual Colonia Nemesio had already spread his red cloth, which was made of baize, measured one meter by ninety centimeters, and was protected from the morning wind by the weight of four irregularly shaped stones, one placed on each corner.

The parlance of street vendors has established codes and norms of behavior obeyed by all in an implicit pact: a red cloth spread out on the sidewalk, in the parlance of the cement jungle, signifies marked territory, established ownership, delineated boundaries for the display of goods for sale.

On the cloth he had placed a tin plate marked "100% Colombian Coffee" and on the plate a large cotton ball and on the cotton ball a kitchen knife.

With the sun at its peak, the office workers ran to punch clocks and the street overflowed with the multitude of unemployed who wander around aimlessly, slowly, up and down, left to right, north to south, east to west, searching for the opportunity of their lives in the promises of lottery ticket vendors, quack herbalists, Hare Krishna disciples of the Guru, evangelists, or militant students.

They drifted along without purpose, day after day, battling hunger and evading thieves, pickpockets, street urchins, those lying on the street with open sores—with stumps, with blindness and accordions—not allowing themselves to be touched or approached by the sad streetwalkers, passing the vendors of stolen watches, of contraband, of colorful trinkets, of things and things and unimaginable things.

When the debris had settled on the street and the day had become a hard fact, Pascual Colonia Nemesio had begun his speech: "Ladies and gentlemen, I am putting this little finger up for sale; observe its vigor, the smoothness of its skin, the cleanliness of its nail, the natural bend of its joints." Still walking, shouting every so often to call the attention of faraway bystanders, he moved the little finger of his left hand.

"What's this nutcase up to?" the people starting to crowd around asked themselves. Some pickpockets took advantage of the commotion to dip into the pockets of the distracted individuals who, with wide-open mouths, followed the interminable hopping around of the little finger.

"Yes, ladies and gentlemen, I am selling this finger so as to buy myself something to eat: I will now put it on this plate for whoever wants to buy it." Pascual Colonia Nemesio removed his shirt and tied it around his head like a pirate; he removed his shoes and his socks, and he rolled up his pants and looked like a shipwrecked sailor in the midst of the sea of people that had begun to form a whirlwind of craning heads and whispers: *This nut job says he's going to sell his finger . . . 'cause he needs food. . . . There's the knife; my God, what if he kills someone? . . . What an idiot: he's lost his marbles. . . .*

With a scream he jumped onto the red cloth, squatted, picked up the knife, and brandished it, making the circle of spectators widen. The onlookers were no longer laughing. The crowd spilled over the sidewalk and began to pour out into the street; cars passed by slowly and the drivers looked on with curiosity, asking, "What's going on? What's going on?" "Some nut case is going to cut off his finger to sell it," they were told. The crammed microbuses leaned to that side when the passengers gathered in front of the windows to see, like a flash, the gleam of sun on the blade of the knife, Pascual Colonia Nemesio's jump, and his scream of pain that pierced through all of Tenth Avenue and zigzagged through teeming streets as the finger fell onto the plate and continued to move for a few seconds, leaving a red stain ("like a flower," as a poet would say) on the cotton ball.

The scream was overpowered by the cutting siren of a police car.

The multitude was so large that the buzz of voices expanded and reached the periphery of the tumult, the end of the traffic jam that had begun to obstruct all of downtown, like a stone that spawns an avalanche: "Some unemployed guy committed suicide," said one; "Someone cut off a guy's finger to steal his ring," suggested another; "The police are arresting the vendors and confiscating their wares," said the most anxious; "Bad karma," they said, "The end of the world," they screamed. The revolution had broken out: there was blood pouring down Tenth Avenue.

The action commenced on all sides, right and left, north and south, from downtown to the outskirts, and from the outside to the inside of the uncontrollable multitude. Those who wanted to leave due to the magnitude of the rumors crashed into those who wanted to get closer due to the magnitude of their curiosity.

The apprehension intensified as when a thunderstorm is about to erupt: frantic that her car might get scratched, a woman tried to speed away, started her Renault in first gear, and crashed into a microbus. The driver got off the bus with a rod in his hand, an Indian club a meter long and two inches thick: the atmosphere was ripe for punitive measures.

The police car finally managed to get to where Pascual Colonia Nemesio was hunched over, on his knees on the red cloth, in the middle of the circle of solitude, clutching his stump, which was gushing blood uncontrollably. Two officers with their nightsticks at the ready addressed him: "Let's see your street vendor license. Let's see your permit to sell meat in a public place. Let's see your sanitation permit. Let's see your papers." The man looked up: his eyes were full of tears; his pirate face, spattered with blood, frightened the policemen. "This guy has lost his mind. You're under arrest." Pascual Nemesio uncoiled his body like a cat and sprung at the officers like a panther with his arms wide and his claws extended.

There was a scream among the multitude, there was turmoil, there was action. The stones that kept the cloth on the ground were now flying in various directions: One broke the window to a bakery and the starved reached for the bread. Another broke the panoramic windshield of a brand-new car belonging to an industrialist with a bodyguard who, with the scream "They're kidnapping my boss," inaugurated the midday air with the first gunshots. Another stone hit one of the police officers in the head, obliging him to take out his gun for the second spray of shots of the day. The fourth pebble flew from one side of the street to the other and went right through a vast shoe store window, breaking and dirtying it. Hands entered to grab shoes for their feet.

The microbus driver had some time ago methodically finished breaking the Renault's windows and headlights and was now launching insults—of a rather cruder caliber than that of the driver with the club—at the woman driver. The multitude grew. Bus and microbus passengers disembarked; a few gentlemen opted on the side of decency and gallantly came to the rescue of the woman, who was now crying hysterically, but they were surpassed in number and skill by those pilfering jewelry and watches, as meanwhile more panoramic windshields were being smashed and an all-out looting of abandoned vehicles commenced. Another group shouted for an end to public transport fee hikes and the driver with the club hardly had time to blanch watching his microbus go up in flames.

The looting proliferated; the shouting intensified as did the columns of smoke that rose into the sky in response to the unemployment rates and the rising cost of bread, milk, meat, drinks, and foodstuffs. The flyers flew, excitedly distributed by the militant students as if witnessing a dream come true: "Our time has come, our time has come. Comrades, let us seize this moment," they said, and the unemployed comrades looked at their hands and moved the joints of their fingers, thinking that perhaps what they needed to do was close their hands and make a fist, as if the saying about not all of one's fingers being equal were true, but more true was that there was strength in unity.

Pascual Colonia Nemesio's red cloth, free of the stones that moored it to the ground and soaked in blood, took flight above the feverish multitude. The police requested reinforcements on their walkie-talkies. "What's going on? What's going on?" they asked at headquarters. "The revolution is taking over the city," the police answered amidst the pandemonium. "They're waving a red flag, they're looting, they're setting buses and private vehicles on fire; we need reinforcements; we've detained the ringleader."

At three in the afternoon downtown was still bursting like frying corn. The police were unable to contain the mayhem, and there were barricades. They again requested reinforcements.

Via Seventh Avenue, heading south, from the Army barracks they advanced with their lights on, in trucks carrying counter-guerrilla troops, hardened Army Rangers, big tough men in fatigues, elite forces who were not afraid of anything. Slowly, as if mindful of their own power, they formed a long snake throttled on either end by the Cascabel tanks and the Urutu armored personnel carriers headed for downtown.

From the affluent neighborhoods of the north of the city came the pilgrimage of the upper class; to Seventh Avenue advanced the procession of elegant gentlemen in suits, refined ladies in high heels, with their daughters dressed in white to celebrate the great carnival of democracy, with ribbons in their hair and little flags in their hands: they waved to the tanks, carpeted the road with flowers for the caravan bearing poison, and waved perfumed white handkerchiefs at the haughty soldiers with chests thrust forward, covered with decorations, with firm chins and virile mustaches, with the fearless eyes of urbane roosters under their combat helmets.

What a display of support for economical cars and discount gold jewelry; how marvelous to be alive to witness this historic moment of the strengthening of institutions, of the safeguarding of the Republic, of the impeccable implementation of the Constitution! Farewell, farewell, ye noble soldiers who make the journey downtown, who shall impose order with the tanks! The telecasters sang their praises, the parish priests blessed them, the future Miss Colombia candidates threw them kisses; applause, applause until the last armed vehicle passed headed for the chaos of downtown where one lone, dense, tense, stretched, extensive column of smoke rose.

The riot police dragged Pascual Colonia Nemesio away and in the truck cage they smashed his head with nightsticks and his balls with kicks. Operation Sweep and the Scorched Earth Campaign had concluded by seven in the evening. The copper-skinned jungle Army Rangers, the storm-troopers, wound up their "ratissage" (rat extermination, as the French call it) and summarily executed all of the prisoners who wore new shoes, more than one watch, or more than two rings; they sentenced to life in prison those whose mouths smelled of fresh bread or who had full stomachs and roast chicken breath, to twenty years in prison those who could read, and to thirty years those who could write.

Cranes removed the shells of burnt vehicles and truckfuls of cadavers were made to disappear in the Brigade crematorium.

The president appeared on television at nine o'clock p.m. and said that he would never hesitate to reestablish the order that had now been reestablished; to restore the calm that had now been restored; to punish the perpetrators who were now detained; to make everyone respect the lives, property, and dignity that had been disrespected. "We have the agitator, the perpetrator who has acted upon imported ideas." The commander in chief spoke and spoke until the entire country went to bed with their hearts at peace and a smile on their lips.

Pascual Colonia Nemesio appeared on the news the following day with his face swollen from the blows and his left hand bandaged: they had sewed his finger back on to discredit the hearsay that had been circulating, to refute those rumors propagated by the subversives, to silence that macabre version of events that stated that all he wanted was to sell his finger in order to get something to eat.

Brides by Night

Evelio Rosero Diago

The things that happen to us!

Right now, for example, some men come to the store, all dressed in gray overalls, and select us from among at least a hundred mannequins. We're both the same height, bald and white, and our cheeks are pink, our eyes blue, and our nails are painted. They put us in a van and after a tumultuous ride we arrive at a ladies' clothing and perfume shop. They install us in a display window decorated to be like a church: marble angels, bibles, candles, roses, a platform, and steps going up to it. Two women come up to the window and examine us. They move us around and then they change their minds, so we end up in the same place as before. And they lovingly decorate each of us with bridal gowns: there is so much love in the women's touch that it's as if they were dressing themselves for their own weddings. They don't leave out the smallest detail. Because of them, because of their love, we have golden hairs on our pubis, soft eyebrows, and sumptuous hair, and they cover us with the most exquisite lace and silk, those of a virgin who deserves the best of everything. Some passersby stop to scrutinize us enthusiastically from the outside. We are perfect: two brides on the threshold of marriage. The women leave the display window and we are alone, before the altar. It's as if the organ had begun to play and the candles glowed and the passersby entered unseen into our church and took communion with us, in coattails, and kneeled at our side, enraptured by our whiteness.

Our ensemble is complete. We have pink garters. And gold chains encircle our ankles.

Night falls and a great black automobile parks in front of the display window. The chauffeur opens the back door. A very old gentleman with a felt hat and a cane steps out and stares at us, enthralled. He enters the shop and tells the saleswomen that he wants to purchase the bridal gowns *and you may as well throw in the mannequins.* He says that money is no object. The two women consult with the manager. We listen, astonished. We've been purchased. The gentleman with the hat pays; he leaves the shop and gets into the great black automobile. His impatient face leans out the window. "Here," he says. The two women carry us, one by one, with adoring care, and they insert us through the window, dressed in bridal gowns. The gentleman with the hat lays us down on his lap. When the automobile starts moving the gentleman's trembling hands reach under our gowns and touch our buttocks, our legs, between our legs, and between our breasts. He unties the bows; he slaps us lightly. His swift, burning slaps make us blush. "What delectable brides," he says. And he orders the chauffeur to accelerate. The chauffeur's eyes sparkle. He also watches us through the rearview mirror: one of us— after the gentleman's inspection—has ended up with a breast outside her gown, as if a fruit had popped out, and the chauffeur sees it and nearly crashes. So the gentleman arranges our garments, and he covers us lovingly, as if to protect us.

We stop at a mansion in the suburbs. A group of very old gentlemen receive us like elated penguins: they take us to a gilded parlor full of mirrors and brightly lit lamps, they sit in a circle and take turns holding us tenderly in their laps. They kiss us very softly on our ears, on our behinds; they caress us and they moan. This delicate act continues for several hours; their gentle moaning intensifies, intensifies into a roar. Finally they slap us, they hurl us among them, as if we were dolls, and in the course of so much flight our gowns lift up and they peer at us and explore us as if we didn't notice, and they give us champagne to drink and the champagne spills all over our breasts, and they tear off our garments amidst biting and smacking, and they fight over us but then they smile and insult us as if they've abhorred us from the moment they were born, and they rip us to pieces with their kicking; they rend us open until we break, such that our arms and legs and heads end up in disarray, in a heap. Her eyes gaze at me, and mine at her. One of us weeps.

The Sixth Commandment

Juan Fernando Merino

I got to know pain and the automobile all in one day. That is, the inside of an automobile and a pain I felt all over. And it's a good thing Aunt Guillermina hasn't found out. Because she's warned me lots of times. Every morning, while I gather my books and my pencils, she says, "Girl, stay away from men because they're all alike. All they want is to disgrace you and as soon as they get what they want they throw you away like an old rag and go looking for some other stupid girl." "Yes, Aunt Guillermina," I answer, and I go to school with my eyes glued to the ground so as not to give them the opportunity to undress me with their stares. That's what Mother Superior says: that the Devil has put little lanterns into men's eyes so they can undress women and weaken their Christian chastity.

My devil had been hiding, but at the beginning of the school year it started to chase after me during the eight-minute walk from my house to school and especially during the eight minutes from school to my house. That's when there are the most lanterns walking the streets of the town and gathered on the street corners saying nasty things and thinking wicked thoughts to weaken us from head to toe.

The devil leaves Aunt Guillermina alone now, but she is tormented during those sixteen minutes when I'm in constant danger. . . . Well, fifteen actually, because despite her limp, she waits for me at the corner every day.

Every day. Because although her body is sickly, her will is still firm. Very firm. Despite the good Lord having put her to the test so many times.

The sad thing is that I'm the one who has suffered through the most difficult test of all. Yes; because on the last day of my vacation Aunt Guillermina decided to calculate time and distance. That morning she said, "Girl, bring me the clock from the living room because we're going to establish at exactly what time you have to be coming in this door." We bolted out the door and my aunt crossed the town at breakneck speed, dragging along her fat legs as if she were being chased and without stopping even to wipe the sweat off her face. Result? . . . Eleven minutes from the house to school and nineteen from the church to the house. When she finished the measurement my aunt wrote down her calculations in a notebook, subtracted 30 percent because my legs weren't sickly, and then she had to go lie down because her body was in agony.

That 30 percent hurt me a lot. I used to dawdle along the way, what with all the trees and birds and flowers, and I would sit on the edge of the bridge to watch the fish swim, but since that day, I have so little time that I'm always in a hurry; I don't greet anyone anymore and sometimes I even have to run the last couple of blocks.

I'm never going to forget the measurement. Because that was the day I saw Carlos Aníbal for the first time, next to the store, with his white apron, so clean, so starched, and because in her effort to snatch away my time, Aunt Guillermina twisted her feet and never walked straight again.

Carlos Aníbal is an apprentice at the Golden Grain, which is ten minutes from my house, which means five and a half minutes from the church because the store is on the way to the church. When he realized that I passed by the store every Sunday, he began to wait for me before and after mass. On my way into the church he just waved to me, but afterward he walked with me until we saw Aunt Guillermina's dark shadow at the corner near the house. He couldn't come to mass with me because Doña Hortensia is in charge of waiting for me in the vestibule of the church. After mass I have to check in with Doña Gertrudis. Since she lives near the church I have to stop by her house and say, "Good morning, Doña Gertrudis, mass is over." "Alright, my dear, now go straight home and don't accept candy or gifts or anything from anyone. And don't you dare talk to any men." "Yes, ma'am, no, ma'am." But the thing is, Carlos Aníbal was not a man. He was Carlos Aníbal.

At first he hardly even looked at me because he was embarrassed. Then he looked. And he brought me candy, wild flowers, and poems that he wrote for me. There was one that went "You are like the breeze of the serene valley." And on the next line: "that fills the countryside with fragrance." I liked that one a lot and I put it in my geometry book next to a sweet-smelling violet. Sometimes he gave me chocolates that he borrowed from the Golden Grain. "Just two or three, Carlos Aníbal," I would say; "I have to eat them on the way and if I'm not hungry, Aunt Guillermina will think that I've accepted food from strangers."

"Sermon?" She asks me every Sunday as soon as I get to the corner. "The Christian family or the dangers of the flesh or the construction of a larger and more comfortable church," I answer, for example. But at that time my head was always in the clouds when I answered her, because I was still thinking of Carlos Aníbal. And it scared me, it scared me a lot because at school they make us recite the commandments every morning and the first one is to love God above all things and I sinned because I kept thinking of Carlos Aníbal and I would forget all about Father Acevedo's sermons as soon as I told them to Aunt Guillermina.

Mother Superior explained the commandments to us at the beginning of the school year. Especially the Sixth Commandment, which is the worst sin of all, the dirtiest, and it must be the longest too because it starts with a wicked thought and ends in eternal damnation. And it's because of the Sixth that all of this has happened. Yes, because on the seventeenth of October, Sister Clemencia, the nun who teaches sewing and decorum, looked through our satchels and desks and she put everything she didn't like into a pile in the middle of the patio and set it on fire to purify us of the sins of the Sixth.

All of the romance novels burned in the bonfire; the fashion magazines burned; the photos of movie actors burned. And the poems Carlos Aníbal had written me, which I had hidden in a corner of my desk in a sky blue folder with orange borders. But that wasn't the worst of it. The worst was that the nuns sent a letter to every home with a list of sinful objects that the abovementioned student had introduced onto school grounds thus transgressing the disciplinary norms set forth by this teaching institution. . . . Ay, Aunt Guillermina! What fury! What screams! I even thought she might die of anger and then I'd have to go live with Aunt Alicia, who since she did have healthy legs would wait for me outside school, outside the church, and even outside the corner store when I was sent to buy aspirin.

Aunt Guillermina didn't die, but she yelled until she was hoarse, she insulted me, she scorned me, she called me libertine, irresponsible, and scatterbrained, and she also said that I had played around with our family honor. And it was no use trying to explain that this was not a game, that Carlos Aníbal truly loved me, that he was the only person in the world who understood me, and that we were going to get married someday. It was no use. And she warned me that if that boy and I exchanged one word, just one word, she would immediately lock me up in the Franciscan convent.

We couldn't talk, but on Sundays when I passed by the Golden Grain, Carlos Aníbal leaned out of the second floor window, blew me kisses, and gestured for me to pick up the letters. He hid them a little up the road, behind an apple tree.

He told me lots of things in his letters: that he dreamt about me, that he was taking a correspondence course in accounting, that his older sister had been to the capital, that he'd marry me even if he had to wait a lifetime, and that Javier had been secretly teaching him how to drive the store's automobile. "I can already steer," he wrote me one week. "I can start it, and turn it off, and I know how to use all the buttons," he wrote in another. And one Sunday he wrote in really big letters: "Now I just have to learn how to put it in reverse, the automobile will rescue us from this prison of love."

I explained to him that he was crazy, twirling my finger next to my head. From his window Carlos Aníbal laughed and moved his arms real fast as if he were driving on a very curvy road.

The week before the train he wrote, "Next Sunday after mass, I'll be waiting for you in the automobile behind the church to go for a ride. Don't worry. We'll be back in time for your aunt."

I was anxious and uncertain that whole week: No, yes, no, yes, no, yes, no way in the world, maybe, I'll be expelled from school, my Guardian Angel finds out about everything, and so does Aunt Guillermina. I didn't eat, I didn't sleep, I didn't study, I couldn't think straight. And on Sunday before mass, I still didn't know what to do. But I made up my mind after hearing Father Acevedo's sermon. He said that we had to fulfill our obligations to the church and keep up with our offerings to make sure we were always in God's grace. Because death could come upon us when we least expected it. Ay! I didn't want death to come upon me so soon. Before I could say good-bye to Carlos Aníbal. Before seeing the inside of an automobile. And much less in disgrace, and so I put all of my coins into the stick with the black bag that the altar boy passed around and when Father Acevedo finally said that we could go in peace, I ran out of the church and across the street and arrived at Doña Gertrudis's house in no time. "Mass is over." "Alright, my dear, and now go straight home because the devil runs loose day and night and doesn't even respect the Lord's day."

Carlos Aníbal was waiting for me. As if he had guessed what Father Acevedo was going to say. I got in and curled up on the seat. We were going at full speed. Carlos Aníbal jumped whenever we hit a stone on the road; he breathed loudly and kept looking around: ahead, then at his watch, at the needles and numbers under the steering wheel, at my hair that was all mussed up, again at the needles, again at the road ahead, again at my hair . . . "You can look now," he said. I lifted my head, slowly, but then I lowered it like a lightning bolt because Mother Superior was chasing us, enraged. "Oh!" I screamed, and I hid between Carlos Aníbal's legs. "Careful, not there; what's wrong?" he yelled nervously. "Mother Superior is coming," I said, terrified. Then we must have turned off of the road because we jumped like crickets and the insides of the automobile were making a lot of noise. We stopped. Carlos Aníbal looked out the window and said that no one was chasing us, that I must have had a fever, and then he started to look for my fever all over and the more he couldn't find it, the more it drove him crazy and the more he looked for it. I was cringing and frightened, but then I heard the eleven o'clock train and that made me happy. . . . I reached out with my hands, with my arms . . . it was approaching from very far away, chugga chugga chugga chugga chugga chugga, and it howled to let the smoke out of the chimney. It was getting closer and closer; the sky went pink, the trees moved, the earth trembled, and I wanted to fly to the conductor with the green cap who has been everywhere and who has strong arms from waving to all the little girls and boys waiting for him next to the tracks. "Faster, Mister conductor, faster, faster," I yelled . . . but at that moment I realized that it wasn't the conductor but Father Acevedo who was pointing at me with a fat finger for the whole town to see. The train was full: Aunt Guillermina was threatening me from one of the windows with a straw broom, and then came Doña Hortensia and Doña Gertrudis and Sister Teresa and Sister Clemencia with a photograph of hell and the altar boy with the long stick from the church. I was so distraught that I was going to ask Carlos Aníbal for help, but I couldn't because the devil had punished me, he had spoiled everything and had put little lanterns into his eyes and then it wasn't Carlos Aníbal anymore because now he was a man and I scratched him; I hit him with my hands, my fists, and my feet and then I threw myself onto the train tracks and the eleven o'clock train ran over my arms, my legs, my ankles, my throat, and my stomach, and I felt a horrible pain all over. I closed my eyes as tight as I could, until they burned, and when I opened them again, the person who used to be Carlos Aníbal was telling me to get out of the automobile because we were almost there. And not to worry. That I had a minute and a half to spare.

I ran to the corner and from there I saw Aunt Guillermina's shadow. I used the minute and a half I had left to fix my hair and my dress. I arrived right on time. "Sermon?" She yelled. "The three enemies of man," I answered, and rubbing my stomach, I lied that I had to go to the bathroom and hurried past her to lock myself in the bathroom and cry.

Contributors

Translator and compiler

Jennifer Gabrielle Edwards was born in Washington, D.C., in 1971. She has published translations in *Michigan Quarterly Review, Metamorphoses, Creative Nonfiction Magazine, Indiana Review,* and *BorderSenses*. She has also translated several novels, screenplays, essays, collections of poetry, and numerous short stories. Ms. Edwards has lived in Spain, France, and Colombia and is currently a patient representative and Spanish medical interpreter living in New York City.

Foreword writer

Hugo Chaparro Valderrama was born in Bogotá in 1961. He is a writer, literary critic, film critic, and journalist. He attended the Iowa International Writers' Workshop in 2002 and has published the novels *El capítulo de Ferneli* (1992) and *Si los sueños me llevaran hacia ella* (1999); the collections of essays *Lo viejo es lo nuevo y lo nuevo es viejo* and *Todo el jazz de New Orleans es bueno* (1992); and two books of poetry that have been awarded the National Poetry Prize of Colombia: *Imágenes de un viaje* (1993) and *Para un fantasma lejano* (1998). His latest book is *Del realismo mágico al realismo trágico* (2005).

Collaborator and author

Juan Fernando Merino was born in Cali in 1954. This writer, journalist, and literary translator has won several short story awards in Colombia as well as a writing grant from the Colombian Ministry of Culture. In Spain he won seven short story awards, including those from Bilbao, Ponferrada, and León. Merino is the author of the short story collection *Las visitas ajenas* (1995) and the novel *El intendente de Aldaz* (1999), and he edited and translated an anthology of contemporary American short stories entitled *Habrá una vez* (2001). For ten years he was the director of translators for the International Film Festival in Valladolid, Spain, and for many years he translated fiction by such authors as Mark Twain, Daniel Defoe, Herman Melville, Roddy Doyle, Coraghessan Boyle, and Julie Hecht. Merino is currently a journalist at *El Diario/LA PRENSA* newspaper in New York. Juan Merino wrote the head notes for this anthology and also has one story included here.

Authors

Juan Carlos Botero was born in Bogotá in 1960 and studied literature at the Andes, Javeriana (Bogotá), and Harvard universities. In 1986 he won the most prestigious story award in the Spanish language, the Juan Rulfo Short Story Prize, for "El encuentro" and in 1990 he won the Latin American Short Story Prize for "El descenso." Botero is the author of a collection of short-short stories, *Las semillas del tiempo* (1992), which was a bestseller in Colombia; a collection of stories, *Las ventanas y las voces* (1998); and two novels, *La sentencia* (2002) and *El arrecife* (2006). Botero has been a columnist for major Colombian newspapers including *La Prensa, El Tiempo,* and *El Espectador,* and has written for the magazines *Cambio, Cromos, Diners, Gatopardo,* and *Semana.*

Álvaro Cepeda Samudio was born in Ciénaga in 1923 and died in New York City in 1972. Cepeda Samudio was a journalist and writer belonging to the "Barranquilla Group" of writers along with García Márquez, among others; he published several stories in the group's literary magazine, *Crónica.* In 1949 he moved to New York City to study journalism at Columbia University. After returning to Barranquilla, Cepeda Samudio became editor in chief of the newspaper *Diario del Caribe* and columnist for *El Tiempo* and *El Heraldo* newspapers. García Márquez wrote that Cepeda Samudio's *Todos estábamos a la espera* (1954) is the best collection of short stories ever published in Colombia. The collection *Los cuentos de Juana* (1982) was published posthumously.

Arturo Echeverri Mejía was born in Rionegro in 1918 and died in Medellín in 1964. In 1946, then-Lieutenant Mejía embarked on a voyage in a precarious sailboat along the Putumayo and Amazon rivers until after four months he reached the Atlantic Ocean and the Port of Cartagena, where he was greeted as a hero for his courageous and perilous journey. Echeverri Mejía subsequently began his literary career, basing his first work, *Antares, del mar verde al mar de los caribes,* on this voyage, and became a part of the Medellín literary group called La Tertulia, which also included writer Manuel Mejía Vallejo, among others. Echeverri Mejía's most famous work, *Marea de ratas,* concerning the political persecution of the 1950s, was published in 1960. He subsequently published the novellas *Bajo Cauca* (1964) and *El hombre de Talara* (1964); the novel *Belchite* was published posthumously in 1986.

Germán Espinosa was born in Cartagena in 1938. He is one of the most representative Colombian writers of the post-"boom" literary era and has published eight novels, including *La tejedora de coronas* (1982), *El signo del pez* (1987), and *Los ojos del basílica* (1992); seven books of poetry; five collections of short stories; and four books of nonfiction. Espinosa's work has been translated into French, German, Italian, Danish, and Chinese. Espinosa holds a doctorate in humanities and has been a diplomat, journalist, and university professor.

Heriberto Fiorillo was born in Barranquilla in 1952. Fiorillo is a writer, television and film producer, and director for which he has been awarded four Simón Bolívar awards, one India Catalina Award, as well as twelve nominations for television and journalism. In 2002 he published *La Cueva: Crónica del Grupo de Barranquilla* about the "Barranquilla Group," which included Gabriel García Márquez and Álvaro Cepeda Samudio, among others, and in 2003 he published *Arde Raúl, la terrible y asombrosa historia del poeta Raúl Gómez Jattin,* which was a bestseller in Colombia. Fiorillo has written two biographies of *vallenato* singers and three films, which he also directed. He is currently the director of La Cueva Foundation, which fosters and exhibits the work of artists, poets, writers, and musicians and is located in the building that still houses the bar and restaurant where the "Barranquilla Group" met in the 1970s. The story collected here, which was adapted and brought to the big screen by Fiorillo in 1985, won a Focine Award.

Harold Kremer was born in Buga in 1955. He was awarded the Antioquia University National Book of Short Stories Award in 1985 for the short story collection *La noche más larga.* His other short story collections include *Rumor de mar* (1989), *El enano más fuerte del mundo* (2004), *El combate* (short-short stories, 2004), and *El prisionero de papá* (2005). Kremer has edited four anthologies of Colombian short stories and his stories have appeared in eleven anthologies of Colombian and Latin American fiction published in Colombia, Germany, Argentina, and Spain. He is the founder of the National Network of Writing Workshops of the Ministry of Culture of Colombia.

Manuel Mejía Vallejo was born in 1923 in Jericó (State of Antioquia) and died in El Retiro in 1998. Vallejo studied fine arts in Medellín, was a university professor and accomplished journalist, and cofounded the Medellín literary group La Tertulia. He wrote for several newspapers in Central America where he lived in political exile for nine years. The writer was president of the Medellín

Ministry of Culture and publisher of the Antioquia Press, and was awarded an honorary doctorate from the National University (Bogotá) in 1986. Mejía Vallejo published ten novels, seven collections of short stories, and four books of poetry. His novel *El día señalado* won the prestigious Nadal Prize in Spain in 1964, and in 1987 he was awarded the Colombian National Achievement in Literature Award.

Plinio Apuleyo Mendoza was born in Tunja in 1932. He is a renowned journalist and writer who has written for many Latin American and European newspapers. From the 1970s until 1987, Mendoza lived in Paris, where he studied at the Institut des Sciences Politiques; was editorial director of the magazine *Libre,* which published the principal authors of the Latin American "boom" including Gabriel García Márquez and Julio Cortázar; and was cultural attaché for the Colombian embassy. Mendoza cofounded the magazine *Semana,* for which he is currently a columnist. He won the prestigious Plaza y Janés Novel Prize for *Años de fuga.* His book of interviews called *El olor de la guayaba* was translated into 17 languages and his memoir *Aquellos tiempos con Gabo* (2000) is about his long friendship with Gabriel García Márquez. Mario Vargas Llosa contributed to Mendoza's book *Manual del perfecto idiota Latinoamericano* (1996).

Mario Mendoza Zambrano was born in 1964 in Bogotá. Mendoza Zambrano studied Hispanic literature at Javeriana University (Bogotá) and later became a literature professor at the same institution. He also studied literature in Madrid at the Ortega y Gasset Foundation, and taught in the United States at James Madison University in Virginia. Mendoza has published four novels, including *Satanás,* which won the prestigious Seix Barral Biblioteca Breve Award in 2002. In 1995 he was awarded the Colombian National Literature Award for his collection of short stories *La travesía del vidente.* The author's latest book is the collection of stories *Una escalera al cielo* (2004).

Roberto Montes Mathieu was born in Sincelejo in 1947. He is an attorney, journalist, and university professor. His books include *El cuarto bate* and *Tap Tap.* Montes Mathieu is coeditor of an anthology of short stories from the Caribbean entitled *Antología del cuento caribeño* (2003).

Julio Paredes was born in Bogotá in 1957. He has published the collections of short stories *Salón Júpiter y otros cuentos* (1994), *Guía para extraviados* (1997), and *Asuntos familiares* (2000), the novels *La celda sumergida* (2003) and *Cinco tardes con Simenon* (2003), and the biography *Eugene Delacroix: El artista de la libertad* (2005). Paredes has been awarded three creative writing grants from the Colombian Ministry of Culture and has translated fiction for publishers in

Contributors

Colombia, the United States, and Spain. He is currently working on a new collection of short stories and translating Ian Thompson's biography of Primo Levi.

Celso Román was born in Bogotá in 1947. He is a sculptor as well as a writer. Román studied veterinary medicine and then fine arts at the National University (Bogotá) and later won a Fulbright scholarship to study at the Pratt Institute in New York. There, he received his master's degree in sculpture; he has exhibited his work extensively both in and outside of Colombia. Román attended the Iowa International Writers' Workshop and has published over ten books, many of them for children. He was awarded the Enka Award for *Los amigos del hombre* (1979), the Netzahualcoyotl Award of Mexico for *El hombre que soñaba* (1983), the Best Children's or Young Adult Book Award for *Las cosas de la casa* (1998), and the Latin American Award for Young Adult Fiction Norma-Fundalectura for *El imperio de las cinco lunas* (1998).

Evelio Rosero Diago was born in Bogotá in 1958. He is the author of the trilogy of novels *Mateo solo* (1984); *Juliana los mira* (1986), which has been translated into Swedish, Norwegian, Danish, Finnish, and German; and *El incendiado* (1988), second-place winner of the Pedro Gómez Valderrama Prize for the best novel by a Colombian published between 1988 and 1992. Rosero Diago subsequently published the novels *Señor que no conoce la luna* (1992), *Las muertes de fiesta* (1995), *Plutón* (2000), *Los almuerzos* (2001), *En el lejero* (2003), and *Los ejércitos* (2007), which won the Tusquets Publishers Award, as well as the collections of short stories *Las esquinas más largas* (1998) and *Cuento para matar un perro y otros cuentos* (1989). Rosero Diago has also published several books for young adults and children, three of which have won national and international awards.

Darío Ruiz Gómez was born in 1937 in Anorí (State of Antioquia). He is a writer, journalist, and literary and art critic who received a degree in journalism in Spain, where he lived from 1956 to 1966. Ruiz Gómez is the author of the novels *Hojas en el patio* (1972) and *En voz baja* (1999) and the following collections of short stories: *Para que no se olvide su nombre, La ternura que tengo para vos, Para decirle adiós a mama, En tierra de paganos,* and *Sombra de rosa y vino.* Many of his stories have been translated into German, French, and English.

Germán Santamaría was born in Tolima in 1950. He is a renowned journalist who wrote for *El Tiempo* newspaper for eleven years, won five Simón Bolívar Awards for Journalism, and twice was the president of the Bogotá Circle of Journalists. Santamaría published two volumes of nonfiction, *Rostros de Colombia* (1985) and *Colombia y otras sangres* (1987). His fiction includes *Los días* *del calor, Marilyn, Morir último,* and *No morirás,* which won the Latin American Novel Award (Santiago de Chile). Santamaría is currently the editorial director of *Diners* Magazine (Bogotá).

Nicolás Suescún was born in Bogotá in 1937. He studied French literature at Columbia University and went on to receive his master's degree at the Sorbonne in Paris. Upon his return to Bogotá, he became professor of English at the National University. In 1969, Suescún attended the Iowa Writers' Workshop and in 1970 was awarded a writing grant in Berlin. He has been the editor in chief of the cultural magazine *Cromos* and World News Editor for the television program *Noticias Uno.* Suescún has published the collections of short stories *El retorno a casa* (1971), *El último escalón* (1977), and *El extraño y otros cuentos* (1980), the collection of short-short stories *Oniromanía* (1996), the illustrated "anti-novel" *Los cuadernos de N* (1994), as well as several collections of poetry. He has published translations of Arthur Rimbaud, Gustave Flaubert, W. Somerset Maugham, Ambrose Bierce, W. B. Yeats, Christopher Isherwood, and Stephen Crane.

Hernando Téllez was born in Bogotá in 1908 and died in 1966. A writer, essayist, journalist, and literary and cultural critic, Téllez was undoubtedly one of the most notable Colombian intellectuals of the twentieth century. He has been termed an "innate agitator" and a writer whose work consisted of "swimming against the current"; the writer Cobo Borda affirmed that "without Téllez, nothing would have been possible." Téllez wrote for several newspapers, was editor in chief of the magazine *Semana,* and is the author of nine collections of essays and other books of nonfiction. In 1950 his short story collection *Cenizas al viento* (which includes both "Lather and Nothing Else" and "Prelude") was published. Téllez was also involved in politics, as a Bogotá city council member, as a senator (for a brief period), as consul-general to France, and as Colombian ambassador to UNESCO.

Policarpo Varón was born in Ibagué in 1941 and in 1962 moved to Bogotá, where he still resides. He has a degree in education and is a writer and university professor. Varón has published the collections of short stories *El festín* (1973), *El falso sueño* (1979), *Jardín del intérprete* (1997), and, most recently, *Equilibristas* (2002). He has also published the collections of essays *Oficio discreto* (1981) and *La libertad social* (1996), the collection of both fiction and nonfiction *La magnífica tragedia* (1986), and the biography *Manuel Mejía Vallejo* (1989).

The Bonjour Gene: A Novel
J. A. Marzán
Introduction by David Huddle

The Decapitated Chicken and Other Stories
Horacio Quiroga
Selected and translated by Margaret Sayers Peden;
introduction by Jean Franco

San Juan: Ciudad Soñada
Edgardo Rodríguez Juliá
Introduction by Antonio Skármeta

San Juan: Memoir of a City
Edgardo Rodríguez Juliá
Translated by Peter Grandbois; foreword by Antonio Skármeta

The Centaur in the Garden
Moacyr Scliar
Translated by Margaret A. Neves; new introduction by Ilan Stavans

Preso sin nombre, celda sin número
Jacobo Timerman
Forewords by Arthur Miller and Ariel Dorfman

Prisoner without a Name, Cell without a Number
Jacobo Timerman
Translated by Toby Talbot; new introduction by Ilan Stavans;
new foreword by Arthur Miller

Life in the Damn Tropics: A Novel
David Unger
Foreword by Gioconda Belli

1875